LIKE SOME KIND OF HERO

LIKE SOME KIND OF HERO

A NOVEL BY

JAN MARINO

Little, Brown and Company
Boston   Toronto   London

First Edition

The characters and events in this book are fictitious. Any similarity to real persons, living or dead, is coincidental and not intended by the author.

Excerpt from "The Glory of Love" by Billy Hill. © 1936 Shapiro, Bernstein & Co., Inc. New York. Copyright renewed. Used by permission.

Library of Congress Cataloging-in-Publication Data

Marino, Jan.
    Like some kind of hero : a novel / by Jan Marino. — 1st ed.
        p.   cm.
    Summary: Ted Bradford steps on a lot of toes and endures many heartaches the summer he decides he would rather be a lifeguard than a musician.
    ISBN 0-316-54626-7
    [1. Lifeguards — Fiction.   2. Self-respect — Fiction. 3. Honesty — Fiction.]   I. Title.
PZ7.M33884Li   1992
[Fic] — dc20   91-22962

10 9 8 7 6 5 4 3 2 1

MV-NY

Published simultaneously in Canada
by Little, Brown & Company (Canada) Limited

Printed in the United States of America

For Len
and for our children,
Lenny, Chris, and Betsy

[Hero] Each man . . . to somebody.

RALPH WALDO EMERSON

LIKE SOME KIND OF HERO

1

It all started with Dan's face. Dan Capra, that is. Miss Barrie, the guidance counselor, came into the cafeteria and headed over to the bulletin board. She hung up a poster, then stepped back to look at it.

The poster looked like one of those old ones where Uncle Sam is looking straight at you, pointing his finger in your face and saying, "I WANT YOU!" Only this time it was Mr. Capra saying, "COME MEET ME ON FRIDAY, JUNE 15, AT 2 P.M., IN THE AUDITORIUM. FIND OUT WHAT IT TAKES TO JOIN THE RANKS OF BAYVIEW'S TEAM OF OFFICIAL LIFEGUARDS."

"Isn't he gorgeous, Miss Barrie?" Bonnie said. Bonnie's the cafeteria's cashier. Actually she's more like a matron at a reform school, always accusing you of stashing Twinkies or something under your tray.

"He is rather attractive," Miss Barrie said. "But Mr.

Capra's physical appearance is not the issue here. It's what he stands for. Challenge. Meeting yet another one of life's challenges."

Miss Barrie is always talking about life's challenges and how life's delivery truck only delivers what one puts into it. She makes me want to puke sometimes.

Will and I were carrying trays over to the hot table when the lunch bell rang. A few of Ray Denson's girlfriends came running past us and over to the poster. I swear it was like Will and I were part of the wall and the picture was alive. The girls actually talked to it. One of them told him he was better looking than Denson. "Really. You are gorgeous." And they all said, "See you later, Mr. C." Then they gazed and swooned until Miss Barrie told them to get in the lunch line.

Lunch room duty really sucked. The kids had food fights and used the trays as missiles when the teacher in charge turned her back. When it was Miss Barrie's day for duty, the lunch room was a real disaster. And Will and I always got stuck with her.

By the time our zookeeper responsibilities were finished and Will and I got to have lunch, most of the kids had gone. Except Denson and a couple of his buddies. "I'm a shoo-in for this," Denson said, looking at the poster. Then he got Jerry Smiddy and Steve Howe worked up, telling them they should go out for it, too. "You know how the skirts go for a lifeguard."

They started to swagger out but before they got to the door, Denson turned. He shook the soda can he was carrying, stuck his finger over the opening and with his overdone Sylvester Stallone pose, pointed it at Will and me. We hit the floor.

"Hey," Denson said, "what's the matter? The drink's flat. I'm just trying to fizz it up."

I got up and when I did, he let me have it right between the eyes.

"Sorry," he said, "my finger slipped."

Jerry and Steve howled.

Will was almost purple, trying not to laugh. By the time he handed me a towel to wipe my face, Denson had split.

"Damn him," I said.

"Quit talking like that," Bonnie yelled over to me, "or you're going to find yourself up in Mr. Fein's office with the rest of the delinquents."

"Sorry," I yelled back. Then I turned to Will. "That does it. We're going to go for it."

"Go for what?"

I pointed to the poster. "That. That's what we're going for."

"What's that going to do for us?"

"I'll tell you what that's going to do for us," I said. "It's going to get us some respect. That guy's picture gets more respect than we do."

Will shrugged. "That's life."

"Well, life's going to change," I said, wiping off the last of the soda from my neck. "The trouble with us is we take things sitting down."

"You were standing up when Denson got you," Will said, stifling a laugh.

"I'm not kidding, Will. We're changing our image."

"Yeah, sure," Will said. "But in the meantime, I've got to get down to the office. Fein wants to see me about something."

"I'm telling you —"

"Tell me later," Will said. "I'll meet you at the bike rack at two-thirty."

I got held up in Spanish and it was almost three when I got to meet Will. He was pacing up and down, stopping every other pace to kick gravel.

"That creep," he said when he saw me. "That slimey creep. I'd like to use his head for a bowling ball."

"Whose head?"

"Denson's."

"What did he do?"

"Remember the class picnic? Remember what that scuzz bucket did to one of the class mothers?"

I nodded.

"Well, I got blamed for it. Somebody told the bus driver that it was my idea to make her think she'd gone deaf."

I started to laugh, but the look on Will's face stopped me.

"I wasn't even in on it," he said.

"Did you tell them it was Denson's idea for everybody to just move their lips?"

"Are you kidding?" he said, pulling his bike out of the rack. "I'm no squealer."

I put my hands on Will's handlebars. "That's great, but where does it get you?" I tightened my grip. "I'm telling you, we've got to change."

"Sure," Will said.

"I'm serious. Can you see somebody telling the bus driver that it was *Denson's* idea to drive Mrs. Frye crazy?"

And before he could answer, I said, "No. Nobody would dare. But with us, anything goes. And you know why? We always take the path of least resistance. And where does it get us?"

"Home in one piece," Will said. "And I've got to get there now."

"I'm telling you, Will, we've got to go for this life-guard thing."

"You're nuts. We'll never make it."

"So we're miserable at soccer. . . ."

"And football and basketball . . ."

"Fact. But we're pretty good swimmers. And with practice, we can hold our own. Face it, Will, swimming is the only sport we don't stink at."

Will pried my hands loose, and started to pedal.

"I'm serious," I said, yanking my bike from the rack. "When that guy comes Friday, we're going to be there. And we're going to sign up. And we're going to make the team. And we're going to be jocks," I said, coming up next to him. "Even if it kills us."

"That's a distinct possibility," Will said.

"Are you in, or not?"

When we got to Will's corner, he said, "I'll tell you Friday."

On sign-up day, the auditorium was packed. I couldn't believe it. Every jock in the school was there. And the girls — there must have been a thousand of them. Will and I finally found a couple of seats in the back row. Mr. Capra was walking around, smiling, and shaking hands with everybody. He *was* good-looking, really built. When he got up on stage and started to talk, I swear the girls' eyeballs popped.

"The Y is responsible for placing lifeguards at your beaches and pools, and we need strong, healthy, young people to join our team," he said. "This is no easy course, but when you've completed the requirements, you'll be serving your community in a way that only healthy young people can."

He went on to explain how the Phys. Ed. Department would be working with the Y in setting up teams. "If you're interested, be at Bayview Beach at seven tomorrow morning. But first, sign-up sheets are on the front table."

That's when the place broke loose. The girls almost trampled the guys trying to get to the tables first.

Will and I made our way down and when we got there, Denson was standing by the sign-up table. He walked over to us and said under his breath, "What's a couple of spastics like you signing up for?"

I pretended I didn't hear him and so did Will. I always felt like a wimp when I did stuff like that. But most of the time it was the only way to handle Denson.

"Did you hear me?" Denson said. "I said, what's a couple of —"

"Get this line moving," Miss Barrie called. "Mr. Denson, have you signed the sheet?"

"Yes," he said.

"Well, move along. Mr. Capra does not have all day."

But before he moved along, Denson got in one last jab: "See you, girls."

"I'd like to punch him out," Will said.

"One of these days . . ."

"Yeah. Sure," Will said.

We were about the last two names on the list. The final bell rang and Will and I headed for our lockers.

"Did you see how many names were on that list?" Will asked.

"So what?"

"So what?" he said, yanking me by the arm, forcing me to face him. "I'll tell you what. They're all jocks."

"Cripes," I said, pulling away. "You are so damn negative."

"I'm not negative. I'm realistic."

"Screw reality." When we walked by the girls' locker room, I said, "Come on, Will. By the end of the summer . . ."

A couple of Junior Varsity cheerleaders ran out of the locker room and headed toward the gym.

". . . we'll be just like the rest of the guys."

Will turned and watched them until they disappeared into the gym. He looked back at me for a long minute, then nodded his head real slow.

"You really think so, Mr. Big Shot?"

"I really think so."

"Okay," he said, "I'm in."

"Aw right," I said, slapping him five. "Let's move out of here." Then the two of us jogged out the door.

2

And that's why Will and I have been sitting at the beach for a hundred hours waiting for our names to be called.

Mr. Capra didn't show up. And when the swimming coach told us Capra wouldn't be coming on a regular basis, some of the girls left.

Mr. Stone called Ray Denson first. Ray was in the water about two seconds when Stone yelled, "Consider yourself Team Captain, Denson." Then he called Jerry Smiddy and Steve Howe.

Denson is part of the reason I've got to make this team. It's weird. I don't even like him. But some part of me wants to be like him. Most of the girls fall all over him. And some of the guys think he's great. And the coaches. They think he's just about perfect. Like

Massive Mueller, the soccer coach. Denson could do no wrong as far as Mueller was concerned. Will and I were on the soccer team's second string last year, and we couldn't do anything right. Especially Will. Mueller was on him all the time.

Will has this habit that drives people nuts. He talks a lot, but when you know him it's kind of understandable. Ever since his father took off, he's lived with his mom, his great-aunt, and his grandmother. No men. Even the dog is female. I swear, they don't give him a chance to say two words a day. Especially his grandmother. She reads all those papers they sell at the checkout counter at the supermarket, and she's always talking about people who diet and lose a million pounds in two weeks and ladies who have babies when they're ninety-two or something. And when she's not talking, his aunt, Marietta, is looking for some lady on an old TV show. "Is that Loretta?" she asks about a million times a day. Will's mom is okay, but she isn't home enough to balance things out.

Well, anyway, Mueller would yell stuff like, "Hey Loughlin, do you ever shut up?" Or, "You want your lips to match the rest of you? Keep on talking and one of these days somebody is going to give you the fattest ones you ever saw."

From that day on, Will was Fat Lips Loughlin to Denson and a couple of his buddies. They had other names for Will and me that I don't want to get into.

My mother couldn't understand why we stuck it out with Mueller. "That man is a bully," she'd say. But she's not into sports, and she definitely didn't understand how much we wanted to be on the team. Any team. Even Mueller's.

Mr. Stone isn't like Mueller. Even I had to admit he was only doing his job when he picked Denson for Team Captain.

Will and I watched Denson congratulate Smiddy when he made the team. Denson banged him on the back and Marty Reddy lifted Smiddy up on his shoulders. And when Steve made it, Denson yelled, "Way to go, Stevie Boy. Way to go."

Then they walked around the beach like they were gods or something, their heads shaved almost bald, talking to the girls, chucking them under the chin. Debbie Harris rubbed Denson's head like it was some kind of crystal ball and she was about to make a wish on it. He had practically every girl on that beach eating out of his hand. The toughies. The silly ones who laughed at every word he said. Even the terrific ones like Mary Beth Atwood and Betsy Dealy acted weird around him, looking at him like he was some kind of hero.

That's another reason I want to make this team and qualify as a lifeguard. I want girls to look at me like I'm something. Not girls like Josette Gormley. Or Norma Elizabeth Frye. But girls who do something else but study. Not girls who carry violin cases with the bow strapped to the side like Josette Gormley.

"Hey, Ted," Will said, poking me, "come back to life. Aphie's in next."

Aphie's this girl we've hung around with since kindergarten. Her real name is Aphrodite. Aphrodite

Morrow. Most kids would shrivel up and die a horrible death with a name like that. But not Aphie. She likes her name. When we were real little kids and somebody made fun of it, she'd go into this whole big story about how her parents met and fell in love under the statue of Aphrodite.

"Aphrodite is the Goddess of Love and Beauty," she'd say. That always got a howl. Aph's okay looking, but definitely not a goddess of love and beauty. She's the kind of girl your mother describes like, "She is going to be a beauty when she comes into her own," or, "She is such an attractive young lady. And so bright." The bright part was true. Definitely. She was the only person in the history of our school to get straight A's from first grade on.

Lately Will's been getting real weird about her. I think maybe he's in love with her or something. I swear being in love with Aph would be like being in love with my mother. She acts about ninety-five and she's always telling Will and me to grow up. "Life is not one big box of Mallomars," she keeps telling us.

"Come on," Will said, giving me a shove, "what's with you? I'm going down to watch Aph."

He started to get up, but I pulled him back. "She doesn't need it and besides, we shouldn't make ourselves too visible. We don't need Denson and his crew messing us up before we get our turn."

"What turn?"

"You're getting negative again."

"Well, I look at it this way. It's three o'clock. We've been here since seven. There are only about ten kids left and we're probably number nine and number ten, and the tryouts end at three-thirty."

"Look," I said, "Aph's in."

We watched Aphie swim toward the buoy. Before she even got there, Stone called out, "Good for you. Welcome aboard."

When Aph got out of the water, she waved over to us and yelled, "I've got to get home. Call me later."

Will started to get up again, but I yanked him back down. "What did I tell you? Let's not get Denson started."

"What'd you say about my friend?" Marty Reddy said from behind us. "Hey, guys, Curlers here wants to get his hair straightened."

Denson gave me that name. My hair used to be straight but when my voice began to change, my hair started to get curly. "Perfectly normal," Dr. Andersen told my mother. "Often happens at puberty."

When I asked my mother what I could do to straighten it, she gave me her usual speech. "Why can't you accept yourself for what you are? Your hair is wonderful."

"But they're calling me Curlers, Mom."

She ran her hand through my hair and said, "What do you care? It's beautiful. Why, Ted, you look like Michelangelo's *David*."

I didn't feel like Michelangelo's *David* now, with Denson's pals sauntering over to me. David's got muscles up to his eyebrows. I've got bones up to my eyebrows. Skin and bones.

"What did you say about being visible?" Will said

14

under his breath. "I swear, if they start something, I am history."

Marty inched over toward us. The rest of Denson's crowd followed. Then he called Denson.

"Geez," Will said, grabbing his clothes, "let's get out of here."

I yanked him toward me. "That's just what they want," I hissed. "For us to quit."

Denson took the lead, moving real slow, like Rambo coming in for the kill.

"I am out of here," Will said.

"You're going to leave Aph here with all these goons, day after day, all summer long?" I whispered. "She made the team."

Denson stood over us. The others stood behind him. He looked down at Will. "The tide's getting low," he said. "Why don't you dive in and raise it?"

Smiddy and Howe had to pick Marty up out of the sand he laughed so hard, like he hadn't heard that joke nine million times before.

"Who does your hair, Teddy bear? Lil's Coiffures?"

Marty doubled over. Will and I held our own.

And then from somewhere, I think maybe heaven, I heard it: "Bradford. Loughlin. Report to the boat. You're in next."

3

"I don't think we made it," Will said, as we pulled ourselves out of the water.

"We weren't bad." I stopped for a minute to get my breath. "We made it to the buoy and back."

"So did Josette Gormley, and she did it faster."

I looked over at Mr. Stone, hoping he'd give us some sign we'd made it. He checked his list, then he motioned for us to come over.

"Hey, guys," he said when we got over to him, "that wasn't bad. Not bad at all."

"Then we made it?" Will said.

"Let's put it this way," he said. "I've got you both on the waiting list."

My heart sank and it must have shown.

"Hey," he said, "don't look that way. I'm being honest. You're okay. But I've got a full complement.

We're only allowed to train twenty-four in all. And you two are the youngest who've tried out."

"What'd I tell you?" Will said to me. "I told you you had to be fifteen."

"A couple of the other kids aren't fifteen yet," I said. "I know for sure Aphie Morrow isn't."

"But they're closer to fifteen than you are, which will make them closer to sixteen by next summer. To lifeguard, you've got to be sixteen. If somebody older is qualified, they get first pick."

He wrote something on his clipboard, then looked over at me. "You've got the build for it. All you need is to work on your torso. Ever lift weights?"

I shook my head. I could just hear my mother's reaction to that one.

"Try it. Nothing too strenuous because you're still growing. Just enough to build up some muscle."

Then he looked over at Will. "You've got the build, too," he said, "but you need to tighten up. Be good for you both to do a little lifting."

He looked down at his list. "Honest, guys, I'd like to put you on, but the regulations are strict — I'm only allowed twelve on my team. Tops."

"Thanks anyway," I said.

"Hey, wait. There's always a chance a few will drop out. One of the girls told me she might get a last minute offer as counselor at Brownie camp. And Chris Leonard tells me his father may be transferred. That'll open a couple of spots. I'll know by tomorrow and I'll call you as soon as I know."

17

Boy, was this embarrassing, not only having to wait for the Brownies and Chris's father to make up their minds, but knowing if we didn't make it, we'd never hear the end of it from the other guys.

We helped Mr. Stone anchor his rowboat and when we were finished, he roughed up my hair and swatted Will on the rear. "Come on, you guys," he said, "it's not the end of the world. I'll call you either way. Soon as I know."

Then he waved, told all the kids who had made it to report at seven-thirty on Monday morning, and he was gone.

"What does he know about the end of the world?" Will muttered.

"Nothing," I said.

Will was right. What did Stone know about feeling as low as an ant? And in front of everybody. Especially Denson. He was standing with his whole army. Waiting.

"Hey, jerks," Denson yelled. "Thanks for the comedy routine." His buddies roared. And some of the girls laughed little high laughs.

"Come on, Will, let's get going."

Will threw me my towel, draped his around his neck, and then the two of us headed for our bikes.

"I'm getting tired of his sick jokes," Will said.

"Things are going to change. Guaranteed."

"You said that before."

"I'm telling you, Stone's going to come through. We're going to be sitting up in one of those lifeguard towers with our muscles having muscles. A million girls running around below us, hoping we'll look down at them." I put my arm around him. "Trust me, buddy. We're going to be sitting on top of the world."

4

Will and I took the long way home. The real long way home. Past Duke's Dairy Bar, where Will had a double hot-fudge sundae and I had a single. Neither one of us was in any hurry to get home and by the time we did, it was about six-thirty.

My father's car wasn't in the driveway and when I put my bike in the garage, I heard my mother in the living room, counting. "AND ONE, TWO, THREE. AND ONE, TWO, THREE . . ."

My mother is a music teacher. She used to teach at the high school, but ever since the budget was cut she teaches at home. She's got the weirdest bunch of students. Half of them have got to be almost a hundred and the rest of them are dumb little kids whose parents must beat them into coming. She used to give me guitar lessons, but she said I aggravated her, so she made arrangements with a man named Mr. Krauss to take over.

"THAT IS WON-DER-FUL," I could hear my mother say. "SIM-PLY WON-DER-FUL. KEEP IT UP."

She had to be teaching Mrs. Stein. The poor old lady couldn't hear what she played, but my mother always told her she was wonderful. And my mother meant it.

"Imagine having the fortitude to work the way she does," my mother would say every time Mrs. Stein left. "Wonderful. Simply wonderful."

I searched in all the cabinets, hoping to find some potato chips or pretzels. Nothing. I looked in the pantry. Nothing.

I wandered into the living room. My mother was tapping her hand on the piano, counting along with Mrs. Stein. I stood there until she spotted me.

"When's dinner?" I mouthed.

She gave me one of her what-have-I-told-you-about-interrupting-my-lessons looks.

I went back into the kitchen and spotted my name on a note on the fridge.

> *Ted —*
> *Mr. Stone called. Meet him down at Bayview Beach on Monday morning at 7:30.*
> *Mother*

I tore it off the fridge, leaped up like the floor was on fire and screamed, "I made it! I'm on!"

"Mom," I yelled, running into the living room. "I made it."

"Ted, I have a student."

Mrs. Stein looked up, confused.

"HI, MRS. STEIN. YOU *ARE* DOING FINE." Then I turned to my mother and said, "When's Dad coming home? I've got to tell him I made the team."

My mother got up from the piano bench and in a fake, calm voice said, "WILL YOU EXCUSE ME A MOMENT, MRS. STEIN?"

"I made it, Mom. I made it. Can you believe it? I made it. . . ."

With her hand on my chest, she pushed me backward through the dining room and into the kitchen.

"Where's Dad? I've got to tell Dad."

"What are you talking about? And how many times have I told you not to interrupt —"

"But I made it. I made the team. That's what Stone called about."

"What team?" But before I could tell her, she said, "No more interruptions."

"I've got to call Will," I said, breaking away from her.

"I'll be finished in five minutes," she said. "Then I want to talk to you. Put some water on for tea. Please."

I dialed Will's number. Busy. I dialed again. Busy. I had just about decided to run over to Will's when I heard my mother say, "YOU ARE DOING BEAUT-

IFULLY, MRS. STEIN. BEAUT-IFULLY. CARE-FUL NOW. WATCH YOUR STEP."

Then she came into the kitchen, smoothing back her hair. "Is the water boiling?" she asked.

"I think so," I said, picking up the phone and dialing Will's number again. Still busy.

"Do you want tea?" she asked, putting a tea bag in the teapot. I swear my mother can make tea for ninety-five people with one tea bag.

I shook my head, picked up the phone and dialed Will's number again.

"Who are you calling?"

"Will," I said. "But it's busy. I've got to find out if he made the team."

"What team? Not that awful Mueller again?"

I shook my head and dialed Will's number. Still busy.

"The swimming team. Mr. Stone's the coach."

"And I suppose he's another fat, balding jock who thinks the crowd is still roaring for him." She squeezed some lemon into her tea. She sighed. "The world is full of them."

"Stone's not like Mueller. He's fair. And when we've passed the course, we're lifeguards."

She shook her head. "The world is filled with lifeguards, too. What it needs are individualists."

"You're right, Mom," I said. "And maybe by the time I'm twenty-five, I'll be the most mature individualist in this family."

She smiled, stirred her tea slowly, picked it up and

took a long drink. Then she looked over at me and said, "What are you going to do about your music lessons, Ted? Did you forget the arrangement you made with Mr. Krauss?"

I didn't answer.

"Did you hear me, Ted?"

"I heard you," I said, not looking directly at her.

My mother's got this thing about commitments. I swear I could be dying, hanging from a tree, shriveling up in the desert heat, taking my last gasp of air as I go down to sea, and if I'd promised her that I'd take out the garbage at seven o'clock, she'd say, "It's seven and the garbage is still sitting in the garage."

"Well?"

"But don't you understand? I made the team. The coach likes me. I can make up the lessons in September."

She definitely didn't understand because she stood up and said, "Ted, Mr. Krauss makes his living on lessons. He depends upon it. You're not taking the summer off."

"But some of your students take the summer off."

"That's different. I enjoy the free time and I'm not entirely dependent on my students. He is. Besides, Ted, you know how Mr. Krauss feels about you."

"And I like the guitar," I said. "You know that. And I'd practice even if I did have the summer off."

She sat down and poured more tea.

"What if everybody stopped coming into the lumberyard all summer? What would your father do?"

I wanted to say that he'd do what he wanted to do

and that was to draw plans for people's houses, but I didn't. I pulled my chair over to her. "Mom, listen to me. This can open up a whole new world. I just read about this old guy — forty-three years old — and every year he goes back to his summer job. He's a lifeguard. A lifeguard at Haley's Beach. All because he's a good swimmer."

"And what does he do the rest of the year?"

"I don't know. But the point is he's got it made."

"Ted . . ."

"Mom, are you listening? I could get to be the best swimmer and pass the Red Cross test and bam, I'm a lifeguard. No more mowing lawns all summer. I could make a pile of money."

"What do you consider a pile of money?"

I didn't answer.

"Ted, did you hear me? What do you consider a pile of money?"

"Well, look at Krauss. He's got to depend on me. . . ."

"What would you like him to do, lifeguard in his spare time?"

"No," I said. "But look what happened to you when the school budget was cut."

"What has that got to do with this?"

"The sports program wasn't cut. Mueller's still there. They even took a special vote and decided if it got cut, the parents would have a drive to get money."

"Oh, Ted."

"It's the truth, Mom. They didn't do that for the music program. There isn't even a band anymore."

She got up and rinsed her cup under the faucet.

I got up and stood beside her. "And another thing, Mom, I have never seen one girl, well, except maybe Josette Gormley, beat down the door of a guy who plays the classical guitar."

She laughed.

"It's not funny. The president of the senior class is on the football team and so is the vice president."

She turned to me and said, "Ted, I'm not telling you not to join this team. What I am telling you is that you've made a commitment and you'll have to keep it."

"Okay. Okay. I can do both."

She gave the cup one last rinse. "And what about that mowing job you took over at Will's apartment complex? You've committed yourself there, too. That by itself is enough to conflict with your lessons." She turned and looked straight at me. "One day, Ted, you're going to come to terms with your talent."

"I will, Mom. But not this summer."

She smiled at me. "Okay. But remember, one goes with the other. No Mr. Krauss, no swimming. Understood?"

I gave her a hug and kissed her. "Thanks, Mom," I said.

"And the responsibility for getting to those swimming sessions is all yours. You know how you are about sleeping in, and I've got early morning students and I don't want any commotion going on."

The last thing I wanted her to do was become a part

of it. I was going to do this myself. I was going to become the best swimmer in Bayview. Then I'd pass the Red Cross course and become the best lifeguard ever. The girls would fall at my feet and Denson would turn green with envy right before my eyes. Just like The Hulk, only powerless. And me. I could just see me strutting across the beach, making my way through the crowd, wearing my official red shorts with the crest that tells it all: OFFICIAL LIFEGUARD. My chest oiled to show off the muscles I'd developed from doing the Australian crawl. I climb up to my official tower and sit down. A million girls flutter below me. Giggling. Waving . . .

"Did you hear me, Ted? I'm talking to you."

"That's fine, Mom," I said. "I mean it's really fine. Me and Will have it all figured out —"

"Will and I, Ted. Will and I —"

"We'll meet at seven or so and ride to the bay. It'll only take us ten minutes or so."

"I thought you weren't sure Will made the —"

"Oh, geez," I said, racing to the phone.

"What have I told you about that kind of vulgarism?"

"Sorry, Mom." I dialed the number. Clear.

And when he picked up and said hello, I knew he'd made it, because I could hear his grandmother in the background: "I just read that too much salt water is bad for you. It can cause the brain to swell and make you crazy. . . ."

"Hey, Will," I yelled into the phone, "what did I tell you? Guaranteed."

"Yeah," he said, "I could hardly believe it when Stone called, but it's . . ."

And before he could really start up, I yelled into the phone, "See you at seven. Seven sharp." Then I put down the phone and yelled, "Okay, all you jocks, move over. *We* are moving in."

CHAPTER

5

The alarm went off and I pulled myself out of bed. I couldn't believe that Monday had come so fast, and that I was actually standing on my feet at six o'clock in the morning. I went into the bathroom, splashed cold water on my face and turned the shower on. I gave Will a quick call and then got under the shower. I stood under the cold water for a long time trying to wake up, and when I finally did, I threw on my clothes and headed down to the kitchen.

I passed my father's workroom on the way. He was leaning over his drafting table. He's an architect, but he doesn't have too many clients. That's why he's still at the lumberyard. He always says that one day he'll sell the lumberyard and open up an office in a big town where there are lots of people who want house plans. I hope he does it soon, because he's old now. So is my mother. She heard me say that once and she almost killed me. But it's a fact. They're probably the oldest parents in Bayview.

"You work all night?" I asked.

He shook his head. "Got up about five or so." He motioned for me to come over to his drafting table. "You remember Dave down at the yard, don't you?" And before I could answer he said, "He asked me to draw up some house plans for him." He held up the plans. "Not bad. Not bad at all."

"Is he paying you for it?"

He shook his head. "If I paid Dave every time he went out of his way for me, I'd be a poor man."

Then he stretched his arms, yawned, and said, "I'll fix you some pancakes. Can't have you leaving the house with no breakfast your first morning out."

I started to say no, and then I remembered how much he loved to cook. Especially pancakes. Terrible pancakes. He made them with butter, fried them in butter, and then served them with more butter. My mother wouldn't eat them, and my sister gave them up when she was twelve. "I've got to watch it now, Dad," she'd tell him, "they're delicious, but they're so fattening."

I tried that one, too, but at five-ten and one hundred twenty pounds, where did that get me?

"Put some weight on you," he'd say whenever he piled them on my plate. "And you know what weight turns to at your age? Muscle. That's right. Good hard muscle."

"Don't make too many, Dad," I said as he started toward the stairs. "I'm not that hungry."

"Emily," I heard him call to my mother. "I'm fixing Ted some pancakes. How many for you?"

"None, please," she said, "but thanks for asking." Then she asked him to close the bedroom door. She couldn't even stand to smell them.

"Esme," he called to my sister, "how about you? I'll make them real thin."

She didn't answer. There are times she plays deaf and there are times she can hear a tiny little fart in a hurricane. And since she came back home, she's been a real pain. She studied voice at the Chicago Conservatory and wants to sing with the City Opera. She tried out for the lead in *Madame Butterfly,* but she hasn't heard if she's gotten it, and she's getting nervous. I'm nervous, too, because if she doesn't get the part, it means she'll be home for the summer, if not forever. I would like nothing better than to see her married. To anyone. Anywhere.

My brother Nathaniel tried to fix her up with his partner out in San Francisco, but she said he wasn't her type. "A podiatrist is into feet," Esme said. "They are definitely not deep thinkers." My mother reminded Esme that Nathaniel was the deepest thinker the family had. Then she told Nathaniel he shouldn't interfere with Esme's love life. But I think my mother would have flown the flag if Esme had gone along with it. "She is so particular," my mother would say. "I wonder if there will ever be a man who'll measure up."

After forcing down the pancakes, I got on my bike and headed down to Shore Road. When I got to where I was supposed to meet Will, he wasn't there. Will's constantly late, but he's always got an excuse ready. Like there was a blackout during the night and his alarm didn't go off.

"Hey, Ted," Will said when he finally showed up. "The alarm didn't go off. I'd still be sleeping if the dog hadn't come into bed with me. Geez, she's getting so old, I think she's losing it. She peed all over me."

"But I called you," I said. "You answered the phone."

"I did? Cripes, I must be losing it, too."

I got on my bike and started down the road, Will behind me.

"I called Aphie last night to tell her we made the team."

"Oh, yeah?" I said. "What'd she say?"

"Not much. I told her to meet us at the corner of Main Street and her —"

"You what?"

"I said we'd meet her. . . ."

I slowed down. "Are you nuts?" I said. "It's already ten after seven and you want to go by for Aph?"

"Yeah," he said. "I want to go by for Aphie. Any objections?"

"You bet there are."

"Since when?"

"Since it'll take us twenty minutes longer. You know what Stone said." I stopped pedaling and turned to him. "You want to start off the first day walking in late?"

"Does that piss me off," he said. "Remember when you had the crush on Denise Doherty and we used to bike all the way down to the Cove and every time we got there, her mother would tell us she just went dancing or twirling? It took us five times longer to get there than it does to get to Main Street —"

"Okay," I said. "Okay."

Aphie was waiting for us at the corner of her street. Will waved so hard when he saw her that he almost fell off his bike. I swear he's getting weird. Lately he's been telling me how beautiful she's getting. "Doesn't she look like Snow White?"

"Snow White?" I said. "Aph's hair is brown. And it's curly."

"Come on," she called as she passed Will and me on her bike. "Do you want to be late the first day?"

I swear, a guy's got to have patience.

We got to the bay about two seconds after seven thirty. Most of the kids were in the water, but Mr. Stone was nowhere in sight.

"Where's Stone?" I asked Kate Elliot.

"He got that transfer he told us about. He's leaving for Minnesota at the end of the week."

"Who's coaching —" but before I finished, I got the answer.

"Seeprise. Seeprise. Seeprise." It was Mueller. Massive Mueller.

I actually felt sick to my stomach. I began to sweat.

I couldn't believe it. How could this happen? He doesn't know diddly squat about swimming and the only way he'd save somebody's life was if his depended on it. The only thing he knew was how to push people around. Especially Will and me. "I'm not staying," I said under my breath.

Will poked me. "Do you believe this?"

"Come on, you two," Aph said and ran toward the water.

Mueller stood up in the rowboat, a bullhorn to his mouth, his belly hanging down to his knees.

"Good afternoon, gentlemen," he bellowed. "Late as usual. But this is *ooonnne* time when that old saying, 'The last shall be first,' just ain't going to happen. Hit the water, you two. And fast."

I just stood there. What was I, nuts? What was I, crazy to spend the summer with him and that big belly pushing me around? There were a thousand other kids sitting in the sand. But it was like always. Just me. And Will.

"You heard me," he yelled again. "Hit the water. Now."

I wanted to turn and go back home but something inside me started to churn. I started to get angry. Real angry. "Okay, fatso," I said under my breath, kicking off my sneakers. "I'll get in the water." I took off one sock and threw it down. "And you know what, fatso?" I tore off the other sock. "I'm going to do it." I yanked off my shirt. "I'm *really* going to do it." I pulled off my jeans. "I'm going to be the best damn swimmer you ever coached." I walked toward the water. "And I'm going to pass the damn lifeguard test and when I do, I'm going to shove that damn bullhorn down your damn throat."

I took a surface dive into the water and swam.

6

"Keep treading," Mueller yelled. "You're all mine until noon." My legs felt like they were going to fall off and my chest ached. But I kept treading.

Will was a few feet away from me. "I'm exhausted," he said. "I'm going to float."

"Don't. You'll rile him."

But he did it anyway. He had floated for about two seconds when Mueller got out the bullhorn and yelled, "Get off your butt and tread, Loughlin, or you're out. That goes for your friend, too."

"I'm treading," I yelled.

"Well, get your chin up out of the water." Then he started to say how important it was to build up the muscles in the shoulders, not the muscles in your head, and if anybody thought they knew more than he did about training, why didn't they get out now so somebody else could get on the team. "You hearing me, Loughlin?"

"I hear you," Will said. And then under his breath, "Jackass."

"The rest of you are doing fine," Mueller called out. "Denson, you're doing good. You, too, Morrow. Smiddy, you're okay. Keep it up."

We kept treading and when Mueller said, "Okay, that's it. Everybody out," you never saw bodies move so fast.

"Take five," he said, "and then I want you to run for fifteen."

A groan went through the team.

"Yeah, that's what I said. That's for starters. I've got you until high noon. You hear me? Running in the sand'll be good for your ankles. And from the looks of some of your ankles, they need more than building. They need replacing."

I wanted to bury myself in the sand before the noon whistle blew. I thought I was going to die. My ankles ached so bad, I could hardly stand it. And Will. He looked like he *was* dead at one point. When the whistle finally blew, I collapsed where I stood. So did Will. But some of the guys kept going. And Aphie. She jogged in place. "Get the kinks out," she said.

"Are you for real?" I said, between breaths.

"Yes," she said, jogging faster. "But you two are pathetic. And you know why?" And before we could answer, she said, "Because you don't get enough exercise."

"Give me a break," I said.

"Give yourself a break," she said. "Exercise. I've been telling you that forever."

"Don't tell me about the Y," Will said. "I hate indoor pools. Especially that one. The chlorine kicks up my allergies."

"It's not so bad now," she said, gathering up her clothes. "I think there's a new maintenance crew."

"Where you going, Aph?" Will asked.

"Home."

"Wait. I've got to rest."

"I can't believe that you two are so grossly out of shape."

"Believe it," I said.

"I need some water," Will mumbled.

"After all that water, you want more?" I said. "I need to have some transfused out."

Aphie shook her head. "The snack bar isn't open yet," she said, looking down at Will, "but maybe the matron has some paper cups. I'll go up and ask."

"Get big ones," Will called after her.

"God," I said, "she's not human. She's not even sweating."

I got to tell you, it made me feel bad. Her muscles were in better shape than mine.

"I feel as though I just walked to California and back," Will said.

He stretched out on the sand, but I got up on my feet and started to jog in place. "So do I, but I'm not going to let anybody know it. And if I can do it, you can do it."

But he didn't move and when Aphie came back with

the water, he gulped it down and stretched out again.

Denson jogged by, his radio blaring, his entourage following him. He stopped and looked down at Will. "Want me to call an ambulance? Or do they let beached whales ride out with the tide?"

I guess Will was trying to impress Aphie because instead of shutting up, he said, "Why don't you dry up?"

Denson pushed Will's leg with his foot. "You're the one who needs drying. You look like you swallowed the bay and it landed in your belly."

"You are such a riot, Ray," Denise Doherty said.

"Hey," I said, "lay off."

"And who's going to make me?"

I looked at him, then over at Aphie. "Me," I said. "That's who's going to make you."

"Grow up, Ted. You, too, Ray," Aphie said. "Mueller won't put up with fighting." She looked over at me. "Let's go for a swim."

"Yeah, Bradford, take a little swim. Aphie can teach you how to kick."

And before I could kick him, Aphie shoved me in the direction of the water. "You're doing just what he wants you to do. Ignore him."

"How can I ignore him? Take a look at Will."

"He can take care of himself," she said, pulling me by the arm. "He wasn't as upset as you were." She gave me one final push. "I'll race you to the buoy."

"Forget it," I said, sitting down in the water. "I'll wait here."

She swam for a while then she headed toward shore

where Will was waiting. I followed. She picked up a towel and began to dry herself. Will sat up and watched her, a dumb look on his face.

When she had finished, she looked over at me and said, "We probably will have to take a CPR course."

"A what?" Will said, shoving his feet into his sneakers.

"A cardiopulmonary resuscitation course," Aphie said. "You have to take it before you can be certified in lifesaving."

"Cripes," Will said, "when do we find the time for this? We practically signed our names in blood with Mr. Sozio." He looked over at me. " 'There is no mowing job too big for T and W Lawn Services,' " he said, mimicking me.

"Calm down. I'll think of something."

"That's easy for you to say. It's not your neck that's hanging in a noose. You won't have Sozio breathing down your back when the work doesn't get done."

"Don't worry. I'll figure something out."

"You should have figured it out before you took the job," Aph said, folding her towel. "That place is huge."

"Do you take lessons from my mother?" I said. "And I don't mean piano lessons."

"Oh, shut up," she said. But she smiled.

We dropped Aphie off and headed for Will's. He lives at the Wexford Arms. He hates it. Even though they rent the largest apartment in the complex, they're still crowded. When his dad was home, they lived in a house, and Will's grandmother and his aunt lived in an apartment over the garage. Will's mom is always saying that she's going to make other arrangements, but Will says he doesn't believe it will ever happen.

When we got there, Will spotted Mr. Sozio by the pool. We took off in the other direction. Fast. From the lobby window all I could see was grass. It was depressing. The place *was* huge. "I can't believe the superintendent gave you and Will the responsibility for mowing that entire place," my mother had said when we got the job. "That's not going to be easy."

And it wasn't. We had two mowers, but only one had any power, and last Saturday after mowing for five hours, we had barely made a dent in it. Mr. Sozio was okay about it, but Will's grandmother kind of likes Sozio, so she was at us for the whole five hours.

We were beat at the end of the day, and when we decided to go into the pool, she said, "Make sure you take a trip to the bathroom before you go in."

Is that typical? Like guys have to be reminded. I'll bet if Aphie had been there, she wouldn't have said that to her. Women are all the same. Esme could be sitting in the car for two days and my mother would never ask her if she had to go. But me? I barely get my foot in the door and she says, "Ted, do you have to?"

Will's aunt was watching television when we got there. She kept asking Will about Loretta Young. "No, Auntie, that's not Loretta," Will said about a hundred times. He's really patient with her. And his grandmother. Most of the time.

Will made us milkshakes that were so thick we had to spoon them out of the blender. And when he started to make the sandwiches, his grandmother kept telling him to make sure not to get the oil from the tuna fish on his hands. "I just read that it causes warts."

When Will and I laughed, she told us we were ignorant and that we should do more reading.

We ate fast and when we were finished, I helped Will clean up. We were just about ready to do the mowing when the rain started. I hung around for a while, hoping it would stop, but when it didn't, I decided to head for home.

My mother had another one of her pupils in the living room. Miss Sullivan. She was about a hundred and five. I could hear my mother telling her she was doing fine. "Why, you'll be ready for a recital come September. Keep up the good work." My mother walked her to the door. "Now you be sure and practice, and I'll see you next week."

When she closed the door, I said, "If she lives that long."

My mother has no sense of humor. She gave me one of her looks and said, "I don't think that's funny. And I don't like you poking fun at my students." She turned and went into the living room. "I'm expecting Carol Fenton in a half hour so please make yourself scarce. And no comedy routines."

I went up to my room and even though I was tired, I decided to get my guitar out. I sat on the edge of my bed and tuned it. Then I rubbed the surface with the special cloth Mr. Krauss had given me. I played some James Taylor. I love his stuff. The melody. The words. It relaxed me so much, I felt like sleeping. I flopped back on the pillow, but every time I moved my head, something crackled in my ear. It was a note. From Esme.

Ted —
  Aphie called. She said she has something to tell you and asks that you call. Please make it brief. I'm expecting a call from the director of the City Opera and I don't want to miss it —
    Esme.

I dialed Aphie's and when she got on she said, "Guess who answered the phone when I called the Y about the CPR course?"

"Dracula. He needs to be resuscitated."

"Capra. I mean Dan. He is *so* nice. He told me to call him Dan."

"What's he doing answering phones? I thought he was a big shot up there."

"I don't know about that, but remember I told Will they must have changed the maintenance crew? Well, they did, and he's in charge."

"Not bad."

"He said anybody who's taking the lifeguard course can use the pool."

"What did he say about the CPR course?"

"He said maybe we should wait till we're closer to passing the lifeguard course itself."

"You mean he thinks we're not going to?"

"Is that all you can think of?"

"No. I'm thinking about how much it'll cost. Did he tell you?"

"I didn't ask. But it can't be much."

"Fifty cents would be a lot for me now," I said. "Did you call Will?"

"Yes," she said, "but his grandmother said he was out and she didn't know where."

"That's funny, he didn't say anything to me."

"If he calls you, tell him we're going to practice up at the pool tomorrow after Mueller lets us go."

"You heard Will. It's bad for his allergies."

"And you heard me. The pool's a lot better. It hardly smells at all. Besides, he needs the practice. So do you."

"If you say so, Mom."

"I say so," she said. "Are you and Will coming by for me tomorrow?"

"Be at the corner a few minutes earlier. I don't want to be late again."

"Get off that phone," Esme called. "My career is at stake."

"I'd better get off. Esme's expecting a call that could take her out of town, and I don't want her to miss it."

"Remember to set your alarm," Aph said. "See you at seven."

"Yeah," I said. "At seven."

Then I jogged down the hall, into my room, and straight into bed.

7

I swear I would have slept through dinner and until the next morning if it hadn't been for my sister.

"Mother. Oh, Mother," I heard her call. And then she started to cry.

After a while I got up and opened my bedroom door. The two of them were standing in the hall by the telephone. My mother was looking at Esme like she was going to break.

"There, there now, dear. It's not the end of the world. There'll be other roles for you."

"Not like this. And now I'll end up spending the entire summer in Bayview. And what's in Bayview for me?"

"Richard Burns?" my mother said, her voice rising in hope.

"Oh, Mother, I can't stand him. All he thinks about are his muscles."

"He can't help the way he's built. He's a very nice young man. He's talented and he's —"

"Rich."

"What did I tell you about trying to be funny, Ted?" my mother said.

"And what have *I* told you about minding your own business?" Esme said.

My mother put her arm around Esme. "Now, now, dear . . . You're just upset. How about the three of us going out for a bite to eat? Your father's going to be late."

Whenever anything goes wrong, my mother suggests going out to eat. "In public, people behave as if what is bothering them isn't bothering them," she always says.

"I'm not hungry," Esme said.

"But I am."

Esme turned and gave me one of her looks. "Look at him, Mother. He's in his underwear. How can you let him go around like that?"

Then, glancing down, she said, "And look at his feet. They're filthy. And to think I'll be here for the summer."

"Boy," I said, "I feel sorry for Richard Burns."

"Whatever for?"

" 'Whatever for?' " I mimicked. "Because he thinks you're so nice and I know better."

"Enough," my mother said. "I've decided for all of

46

us. We're going to Casey's for supper. Do us all good to get out. Esme, you drive, will you?"

It killed me when my mother said that. My mother didn't drive. It was embarrassing, having the only mother in town who didn't drive. But it didn't embarrass her. My father insisted on her taking lessons once, and she did. She failed. "Well, that's that," she'd said.

"What do you mean that's that?" I'd said. "Everybody drives."

"Well, I am not everybody." And she never tried again.

It was mobbed at Casey's and when we finally got seated, starving as I was, I almost lost my appetite. Ray Denson was sitting in the booth right behind us. With Jerry Smiddy opposite him. And here I was with my mother and my sister. Not even my father to balance it out. I wanted to crawl away.

"Let's switch tables," I whispered to my mother.

"I can't hear you. Speak up."

"He says we should switch tables."

"Why? This is a perfectly fine table."

And then the waitress was standing next to us, pulling out her pad, asking, "What'll it be?" After Esme and my mother ordered their usual diet plates, I ordered a couple of cheeseburgers and fries. "And a malted. Make it chocolate."

"What disgusting things to put in one's stomach," Esme said. "Nothing but fat."

Denson turned around with a shocked expression. He shook his head back and forth and mimicked,

"What disgusting things to put in one's stomach. Awful. Awful. Awful."

It was. And I could tell it was going to get worse.

"Oh, leave him alone, Esme," my mother said. "He's growing."

Denson leaned back toward Jerry, puffed out his cheeks, spread out his T-shirt and nodded.

"Is there somebody you know back there?" my mother said.

"Just a couple of guys."

She started to turn.

"Don't, Mom. Please."

She shrugged. "Just wanted to say hello."

Then she and Esme got into this deep discussion about why things didn't work out for Esme and Chicago. Denson kept turning around, and then he and Smiddy would bust up. I knew they'd destroy me at practice tomorrow. They had so much family material to go on.

By the time the waitress brought our food, Denson and Smiddy had left and my appetite had improved. When we were finished, my mother turned to Esme and said, "Feeling better?"

Esme nodded.

"Good. It may not be the summer you planned, but who knows, it just might be one of your best."

But not mine. Between Mueller and Denson and now Esme, it was definitely not going to be one of my best.

I decided to drown myself with another malted and

blueberry pie with ice cream. Esme kept telling me to wipe my mouth and my mother kept telling Esme not to nag, and Esme kept telling my mother how much work my mother had to do on me, and my mother kept telling her we all grow up in our own time. I felt like I was a speck on the table.

"Nathaniel wasn't like this," Esme said.

"Nathaniel was born old," my mother said, looking at the check.

My whole life, I've been hearing how my brother was born mature and how Esme was like a little old lady by the time she was three. I swear every teacher I ever had asked the same question. "Are you Nathaniel and Esme's brother?" And when I said yes, they'd say, "Well, we can't expect siblings to be clones of one another." But we were clones when it came to sports. They stunk, too. But that was going to change.

"Did you hear me?" Esme said.

"Did I hear what?"

"You've got blueberries all over your mouth."

"Oh, Esme, let him be," my mother said, looking at the check. "Do you think a two-dollar tip is enough?"

That's another thing about my mother. She's cheap. Not with everything, but with things like tips. She thinks she's still living in the sixties.

"*Mo-ther,*" Esme said, "it's now customary to leave more than fifteen percent."

My mother sorted out her money and got up. "Come on, Ted. Dad will be home and I want to see how he made out with those house plans."

Denson and Smiddy were standing in the parking lot and when we passed them, I tried to act cool. "Yo," I said. "See you at the beach."

"Don't let Mommy forget to pack your bathing slippers," Denson said.

I should have said something smart. That's my problem. When it's too late, I think of all the things I could have said.

"Were those the friends that were sitting behind us?" my mother asked as she climbed into the car.

I nodded. "They're on the swim team."

"I'm not surprised."

"Why?"

"Their hair."

"What hair?" Esme said. "Except for those obscene little tails hanging down their necks, they hardly have any."

"They've got crew cuts," I said.

"*That* is more than a crew cut," my mother said. "But I suppose that's the way the coach likes it."

"I guess so," I said.

She looked at me and said, "Well, they certainly fit the mold."

"And I don't?"

She smiled at me and shook her head. "You're different."

But that wasn't going to last. I'd make sure of that.

8

When I told Will what Aph told me about using the pool, he definitely wasn't thrilled.

"But Aph's right. We need the practice."

"And when do we work in all the other crap we've got to do?"

"Don't worry," I said. "I'm thinking."

"How come she called you?"

"She called you first, but your grandmother said you were out."

Will came alongside me.

"So where were you?"

"Just out," he said.

"Where out?"

"Out. Just out."

When I told him what Capra had said about putting off the CPR course, he looked relieved.

"That's great, because I saw Sozio this morning and he wants the pool area finished no later than Thursday."

"So we'll do it."

"How?"

"I'll figure something out."

"Sure," Will said, pedaling faster when we saw Aphie at the corner. "You'll figure it out. No problem."

"You'll see," I said. "Besides, I need the money. Esme told me we're giving a party for my parents and I've got to pitch in. With cash."

"How come you're having a party?"

"They'll be married thirty years."

"Geez, I didn't think anybody could be married that long."

"Who's married that long?" Aphie said, turning into the road with us.

And when I told her, she got this real funny look on her face.

"Imagine that," she said, "in love for thirty years."

I never thought of it that way. My parents in love. And for thirty years.

She smiled at me and said, "That's beautiful," and then she began to pedal harder.

It was getting late, so we crossed over the railroad tracks and cut through the eelgrass to the bay. As soon as we got there, Denson made some crummy remark about Theodora forgetting her slippers, but I didn't have time to answer him because Mueller was yelling for us to get in and start treading again.

Then he had us do laps. Two kids at a time. Denson went first with Steve Howe. Much as I hate to admit it, Denson's a good swimmer. His whole body stayed close to the water, like he was part of it.

I wasn't bad, but I wasn't great. I could hold my own, but I wasn't smooth. He was smooth.

"You can do better, Howe. You hear me?" Mueller kept bellowing. And to Denson: "Great going. Show them what style can do."

Even if Denson wasn't such a creep, Mueller's liking him the way he did would make you hate him anyway. Mueller was probably like Denson when he was a kid, only fat. A fat creep.

"Jerk," Will said under his breath when Denson finished up the laps and walked by us.

Mueller teamed Aphie up with Jerry Smiddy and she made him look sick. She was better than Denson. She looked so great, I felt like leaving before Mueller called me.

But I didn't.

I was hoping Will would get called with somebody else. It'd be better for our image. Not that anybody but Will could ever be my best friend, but if Will went in with someone like Nancy Coles, maybe Mueller would ease up on him. And me.

"Okay, now," Mueller said after almost the entire team had been called, "who we got left?"

He looked down at his list and then said, "Loughlin and Bradford, hit the water."

"Damn," I said under my breath.

"What'd you say?"

"Nothing. Let's move it."

When we hit the water, Mueller started blowing out orders. I couldn't see what Will was doing, but I heard. "Loughlin, get your butt moving.

"Your head looks like it's on a swivel, keep it still or I'll get you a head brace.

"Keep those arms close to your body . . .

"Not bad, Bradford. Not bad at all for an old lady, but it's sad for a guy.

"Keep your head close to the water. Stop looking up, you lose time.

"Keep going. I'll tell you when it's time to stop.

"Get those feet moving.

"Are you two ever going to get the hang of this . . . ?"

When he finally let us out, Will was ready to quit. "That horse's ass will never stop," he said.

"Maybe he won't," I said, "but I'm hanging in and so are you."

Will just looked at me.

"Attention," Mueller yelled through his bullhorn. "Tomorrow, report to the beach house at seven-thirty. Sharp. We start using our heads tomorrow . . ."

"I guess he's staying home," Will said under his breath.

". . . so what you have for tonight's assignment . . ."

"Geez," Will muttered, "when do we breathe?"

"Shhhh," Aphie said.

". . . study table 1.1 — comparison of lifesaver and lifeguard roles. All of chapter two on personal safety. And pages seventeen through twenty-one of chapter three. Remember, seven-thirty. Sharp."

"Did you hear that?" Will said.

"Quit complaining."

"Who's complaining? I asked if you heard it. And will you quit acting like a big shot?"

"Shhhh," Aph said.

Mueller blew his brains into his bullhorn for a little bit longer and when he finally let us go, Aph asked us if we wanted to go up and practice for a while. She turned to Will. "Did Ted tell you about the chlorine at the pool?"

Will nodded.

"So let's go," she said. She picked up her things and headed for her bike.

Will looked like he was going to flop, but he wrapped his towel around his waist and agreed to come.

"Hey, Aph," I yelled, "wait up."

But she didn't. She pedaled like she was in a down-hill race, and by the time Will and I caught up to her, she was halfway up the road leading to the Y. The road is beautiful, but it's a bitch to climb — it's curved and uphill all the way.

When we got up there, we put our bikes against the wall of the administration building and went into the reception area. Aph explained to the girl behind the desk what Capra had said, and she gave us pool passes. "Just make sure you shower before you go into the pool. No exceptions."

"I'm taking a quick shower, and then I'm in," Aphie said, and disappeared into the women's locker room.

Will and I headed for the men's section. "Boy," Will said, nudging me, "I'd like to follow Aphie in there. Just for a quick peek. Know what I mean?"

"Are you crazy?"

"I didn't say I was going to do it," he said. "And don't tell me you never think things like that. 'Cause I'll tell you you're abnormal."

"Not about her."

"Who then? Denise Doherty?"

"Dry up," I said, snapping my towel at his legs.

I threw my stuff in a locker and got under the shower. I thought about what Will had said. I definitely had never thought of Aphie like that. Naked. Geez, it would be like thinking about Esme like that. It just wouldn't be right. Now Mary Beth Atwood was different. She is definitely not family. She's got the sweetest butt I ever saw. Not that I've seen it all. Just the part at the end of her bathing suit.

"You coming out today, Bradford?"

"I'm on my way."

The pool was practically empty and it had that silence you don't get anywhere else. Kind of a ringing silence, until you hear a splash. Then silence again until the one who made the splash surfaces and starts to swim. I like it. It's almost like you're in a bubble.

Aphie was walking toward the end of the diving board. She bounced a few times then dove in.

"Geez," Will said, "she *is* changing."

"What's with you? She looks the same to me."

"You need glasses," he said. "You know who she reminds me of?"

"You told me. Snow White."

He shook his head. "Betsy Dealy. She reminds me of her."

"You're the one who needs the glasses," I said.

Aphie resurfaced, shook her head and smiled at us. "Come on in. It's great."

Will headed for the diving board, I took a surface dive. I swam under water for as long as I could hold my breath. It was great being under. I surfaced, took another deep breath and went down again. When my air ran out, I closed my eyes and let my body float to the top.

I heard voices even before I lifted my head out of the water. Will and Aph were standing at the end of the pool with Capra. He had the kind of build I would die for. Tall, but not beanpole tall like me, and not muscle tall like Richard Burns.

"Come on over," Aphie called, motioning to me.

I swam over to them. Capra bent down and held out his hand. "Hey, Ted, how you doing?"

"Okay, Mr. Capra."

"Dan, please." He turned to Aph and Will. "Get in. I want to see what you kids can do."

Will and Aphie dove in and the three of us did some

laps. Capra sat at the edge of the pool, his feet dangling, and when we'd done about five laps, he said, "You guys aren't bad at all." He looked over at Aphie. "Where'd you get your training?"

"Here."

"I'm impressed." Then he looked over at Will. "You need some legwork. Pick yourself up a pair of fins. They'll not only develop your kick, but they'll build up your leg muscles." He glanced over at me. "You, too. Give you more resistance."

He stood up and said, "I've got to do a pool check and get some paperwork done."

"How come you're not at the beach?" I asked. "We thought you were in charge of the whole program."

"Me? In charge of the whole program?" He shook his head. "I'm the alternate lifeguard here. And the full-time summer pool man."

"So how come your picture was on the poster?"

"PR. Strictly PR," he said. "Mr. Crowley's in charge."

"Is that the guy who was down at the beach with Mueller yesterday?" Will said. "The one who looks about ninety?"

Dan laughed. "Well, he's not. He's my uncle and he's forty-nine and unphotogenic. So they asked me to do it." Then he looked back at me. "You'd make better time if you kept your head down. You might even think of getting a cap to keep your hair out of your eyes. It helps."

Geez, that's all I need. I wouldn't be caught dead

with a bathing cap on. It'd be like wearing your grandmother's bathing slippers.

"I'll see you tomorrow," he said, and he was gone.

Will hauled himself out of the pool. "We better get started on the mowing," he said. "Maybe we can get most of the pool area finished by tonight."

"I've got to do something downtown first," I said.

"That's great. So when do we mow?"

"As soon as I get back."

Aphie headed toward the locker rooms, but turned and said, "I'll ride downtown with you. My mother's got a late class and I've got to get something for dinner."

"I swear, I don't know how I got into this," Will said, yanking his clothes out of the locker. "We should have stuck to mowing Mrs. Grainger's place. But, no, you've got to be big time."

"Don't worry," I said, "I think I've got an idea."

"Like what? How to get it to stop growing?"

"Is that all you can think of?"

"Yeah," Will said, "especially since Mr. Sozio is a resident fixture in my building, and you made promises that I'm going to have to keep."

"Will you get off my back? I told you I'd figure something out."

Now all I needed was some time to think.

CHAPTER

9

"Come over as soon as you can," Will said when we got near town. "I'll probably still be mowing the south end."

"Okay," I said.

"And bring another rake with you. The one you brought the other day is busted."

"What happened to it?"

"It was busted when you brought it."

"It was not. It was almost new. What'd you do to it?"

"What do you call new?"

"Stop it," Aph said. "You sound like an old married couple."

"Not me," I said.

Will started to say something, but Aph turned to him and said, "You coming by for me tomorrow?"

"Sure," he said.

"Come by earlier."

He nodded then turned to me. "I'll be waiting for you. Make it fast."

I left Aphie at the butcher shop and headed down Main Street. I'd been considering something ever since the night I had dinner at Casey's with my mother and Esme. I was tired of being different. And now, with Capra telling me I should wear a bathing cap, I knew I had to do it.

I biked down to the barbershop and when I got there, Frank's chair was free. He'd been cutting my hair since I was a kid. He used to tell me how my mother would stand behind him and dictate how much to cut. "Not too much from the sides," she used to say. "Not too much from the top. And leave the front long."

This time I told him, "Cut it off, please."

"Off?"

"That's what I said."

"Does Mama know?"

"It's my hair, Frank."

"This I know."

"Off."

"All off?"

"All but a little in the back."

Frank shook his head and picked up his scissors. "Off," he said.

He swung the chair around and began to cut. Then he used the clipping machine. Hair fell everywhere. Big clumps of it stuck to Frank's shoes. I kept sneezing because the hair was flying around my face. When Frank was finished, he turned the chair around. I used to love it when he did that because the mirrors were set up so you could see yourself about a million times. But this time I didn't like it. With no hair on my head, my forehead looked about two miles high and my ears were huge. And my neck. Geez, it was thin. The little strip of hair in the back looked kind of like a mouse crawling down my shirt.

Frank sighed and shook his head. "Kids. They drive you crazy."

He took the towel off my shoulders, sprinkled talcum on the back of my neck, and brushed me off. "Tell Mama it wasn't my idea." Then he turned and said, "Next."

I was kind of sorry I'd done it. But I had to be practical. Mueller liked short hair, and long hair got in my way. Now there'd be no more wiping it out of my eyes. No more tossing my head back during practice.

I stopped off at the drugstore and even though I didn't want to, I bought myself a racing cap. I figured I'd put it on when I got home. Then after a while I'd take it off and kind of ease everybody into my new haircut.

When I walked in the front door, I knew my mother was in the living room. "One, two, three, one, two, three," she was saying. "There is no way out of counting, Pauline. Absolutely no way. All good musicians count."

I could see my father in the den reading the paper. Esme was nowhere in sight, but when I got to the upstairs hall, the phone rang, and there she was.

"Hello," she said. "Oh, hello there."

Without looking at me, she held her hand over the phone and said, "I would appreciate some privacy."

"You got it."

After I took a shower, I stuck the racing cap back on my head and headed to my room. Esme was standing in her doorway. "What did mother tell you about your so-called comedy routines?"

"What do you mean?"

"Take that foolish cap off your head. You're not even mildly funny."

I pulled the cap off my head and when I did, Esme's mouth opened. Wide. "Oh. My. God," she said. "What did you do to yourself? You look awful."

"You don't like it?"

"Like it? Who could like it? Especially that disgusting piece hanging down your neck."

"All that hair got in my way."

"Mother is going to love this."

"Don't tell her," I said.

"I won't," she said. "It'll be just our little secret." She came over and ran her hand over my head. "It really will be quite wonderful when it begins to grow back. All those little hairs sticking out in every direction." She laughed and went downstairs.

I looked in the mirror in the hallway. I stood on my toes so I couldn't see the part of my head that used to have hair on it. I still could tell I looked different. And boy, could I see my ears.

After a while, I decided to go downstairs. Casually. Not make any big deal about it. Just stroll down the stairs and into the kitchen. I was thinking about whether I should put on the racing cap when Esme came to the bottom of the stairs and said, "Ted, I need some help putting a leaf in the dining room table."

When I came down the stairs, my mother was still counting. I walked through the hall, past the living room, and into the kitchen. Esme was trying to pull one of the table leaves from the closet. "Can you reach?" she said. "I can't." I got up on a chair and gave it a yank and when I did, the whole shelf came down.

"What was that?" my mother called.

"Nothing," I said, jumping off the chair. "Everything's fine."

The dining room door opened. My mother stood there. Motionless. "Oh, dear, merciful God, what have you done? Where's your hair?"

"It'll grow back," I said.

"Oh, good Lord," she said, holding her hands up to her head, "how could you have done such a thing?"

"Mom . . ."

"Hugh," she called, "come quick."

As my father came through the door, she said, "Look at him. Look what he's done."

"Calm down," my father said when he saw me. "It's

not bad." He put his hand on my head. "He's not bald, he's just got a tall face." He picked up the shock of hair from the back of my head. "Maybe you can do what men my age do when they're left with only a few strands." He pulled it up over my head and smoothed it down. "Won't stay," he said. "Use some of Esme's hairspray. That ought to do it."

Then he turned and headed back to the den. "Remember, Em," he called back, "it's only hair. And it's his."

"Stop that. He does not need encouragement." Then she called out to Pauline, "Keep counting."

"Mother, please," Esme said, "Richard will be here by six and I can't get the table to work."

"How come he's coming?" I said. "I thought you couldn't stand him."

"I can't," Esme said. "He called and since I wasn't here, dear old Richard conned Mother into inviting him for dinner." She looked over at me and started to laugh. "Do you know what they call people in Chicago with a head like that?"

I said no.

"Skinheads. That's what they call them." Then she turned to my mother and said, "If you don't do something with him, he'll have his ear pierced next." Then she took the leaf and went into the dining room.

"I'll be back in just a moment, Pauline," my mother called. She came over and looked me straight in the eye. "Does this man wield such power that you feel you have to comply?"

I shook my head. "Mom," I said, "I wanted to do

it. My hair got in the way, in more ways than one. I told you the guys call me Curlers and it got in my eyes in the water."

"That's absurd. You had such beautiful hair."

"It's not dead. You heard Dad. It'll grow back."

"Oh, Ted, Ted, Ted," she said. "When are you going to start cultivating more independent thinking?"

"I will, Mom. But not this summer."

My mother sighed a long, long sigh and walked back to the living room. "And one, two, three, and one, two, three . . ."

I pulled the cap back on my head and went into the dining room. Esme was struggling with the leaf. I got on the other side of the table and worked it in. She looked over at me and said, "Well, you certainly picked a good day to pull this one."

"Why?"

"Richard."

She gave the table one last push.

"I'll eat in the kitchen if you're embarrassed to have him see me."

I thought I saw a smile coming, but she turned and started out to the kitchen. "Thanks for the offer, but no way are you eating in the kitchen. I'm depending on you to scare him off. For good."

I stood there. Shocked. My sister actually said thanks. And in a voice she never used, at least with me. "That's okay," I said. "Glad to help."

My head started to sweat under the cap so I took it off. I went back upstairs and looked in the hall mirror again. I turned my head one way and then the other, seeing things about myself I never saw before. Like my head wasn't exactly shaped the way I thought it would be. It was kind of dented in at the top. And one ear looked bigger than the other. I looked almost tough. I stuck my chest out and flexed my arm muscles. Then I picked up the chair by the telephone and held it over my head.

Esme came up the stairs and before I could get the chair down, she said, "Will you never stop your clowning? It bores me." Then she swept into the bathroom.

I put the chair down and shadowboxed all the way to my room. Things were back to normal. Esme was Esme again. And I began hoping old Richard would find her irresistible. Improbable. But who knows? Aphie told me the other day that there's actually a Mrs. Massive Mueller, so miracles *can* happen.

10

When I looked in the mirror the next morning, I didn't have the courage I'd had last night. I didn't look tough. My head looked like a huge eggplant somebody had painted white. I rummaged around in my closet for my baseball cap, stuffed the racing cap into my jeans, and headed downstairs.

I was starving. I hadn't had anything to eat since dinner. And that was a scene. Richard was a jerk and the biggest phony I ever met.

"Don't you look lovely, Mrs. Bradford," I heard him say, when my mother let him in. "You look younger every time I see you."

And it got worse. He told Esme she was a vision. Then he handed her a bouquet of flowers that was bigger than the piano.

Esme looked like she was going to puke, but she thanked him.

Then I almost puked because he said the most sickening thing I've ever heard. "Esme," he said, "flowers pale next to you."

And all during dinner, he never shut up. He was so busy talking about himself, he never even noticed my head. Or the fact that my mother had burned the roast. Or that my father really wasn't interested in the fact that Richard's father was retiring. My mother said, "How nice." Esme stared into space.

Then he told us he had plans to diversify his father's business. "Do you know what business is really pressing forward?" And when nobody answered he said, "The insurance business." And when nobody asked why, he said, "The facet I find most interesting in the insurance field is the burgeoning of burial insurance."

Esme dropped her fork.

"Surprised? Well, it's the only way people can look forward to a decent funeral these days, what with the price of caskets going up."

"Well," my father said, "I won't lose sleep over that one, Richard. Emily and I have decided to be cremated. Right, Emily?"

"That's right, Hugh."

"I can get you insurance for that, too."

Nobody said much after that. Except Richard. After a while, I excused myself and called Will.

"Thanks a lot for coming over," he snarled. "I mowed for three hours and I didn't even make a dent in it."

"I'll make up the time," I said. "I promise. I've got a couple of ideas —"

"You know what you can do with your ideas?"

"I'm telling you, Will, I'm going to come up with something."

"And I'm going to bed. See you in the morning."

I took out my guitar and started to play. It felt good in my hands. I played some scales and then I fooled around with some Chet Atkins songs. I liked him almost as much as I like Taylor. He can do anything with a guitar. Classical and jazz, even country. Most of the kids won't touch anything he does. Too old-fashioned. But, geez, he's so good. I was just getting into some light jazz when I spotted the lifesaving manual that Mueller had told us to study. I put my guitar down and picked up the manual and started to read. And the next thing I knew, it was morning.

"How come you're up so early?" my father said when I got into the kitchen.

"Mueller wants to get in some early practice."

"How are you doing?"

"Better." I flexed my arms. "Hey, look, Dad. Do they look different? Not so skinny?"

He nodded. "How about some breakfast? Pancakes? French toast?"

"No thanks," I said, reaching for the cereal. "I'm not too hungry."

"Well, make sure you eat enough of that," he said, taking his coffee and heading for the den. "Make yourself some toast, too. And juice."

I shoved the toast in the toaster and poured myself

some milk. I was a little nervous about Will and Aphie seeing my haircut for the first time. Sometimes Will goes too far with his kidding, and there are times Aph thinks he's funnier than he really is. And it can kind of get to a person.

"Ted," my mother called, "don't forget to call Mr. Krauss. He wants you to come at one on Friday."

"How come? He said at two."

"Call him and find out," she said, coming into the kitchen. "And Ted, it's been almost a week since all this began, and I haven't heard you practice."

"I practiced last night."

"I didn't hear you."

"Richard must have been talking," I said.

She shook her head slightly and poured herself some coffee. "Remember your commitment. And that's all I'm saying."

I poured myself juice and sat at the table waiting for the toast to pop up.

"We don't sit at the table with a hat on."

"Sorry," I said, taking it off.

"I'll make an exception this morning," she said, looking down at me.

After giving my mother my solemn promise to come home and practice, I took off on my bike. As usual, Will was late, and when he got there, he looked awful. His face was all puffy and his eyes were slits.

"What happened to you?"

"Nothing."

"What do you mean, nothing?"

"Maybe it's allergies."

71

"But you haven't had them in a long time."

"So they came back."

"Are you okay?" I said. "You really look awful."

"So I look awful," he said. "But you don't look so great either. What have you got that dumb hat on for?"

"I got a haircut," I said, taking off my hat.

"A haircut?" He howled. "You've got no hair."

"It'll grow out before you know it."

"That's what you think. Let me tell you something about hair."

"Don't," I said, and pedaled hard, leaving him behind. I heard him say something about hair follicles and how they grew.

When we got to Aphie's street, she was heading toward us. Before I could tell Will to shut up, he told Aph that she should get me to take my hat off.

"Knock it off, Will."

"Go ahead, Aph. Ask him."

"Why?" she said.

"Just ask him to take it off. You'll figure it out."

She looked over at me and before she asked me, I took it off.

She let out a little scream. Then she shook her head and said, "Who would do something like this?"

"Frank did it," I said.

"I don't mean who cut it. I mean what idiot would do something so disgusting?"

"Denson and his whole crowd wear their hair like this."

"You mean their heads," Will said. "Wear their heads —"

"Don't tell me you haven't noticed?"

She didn't answer. She turned and pedaled toward the bay.

"Geez," Will said, following behind me, "you've got a great pair of ears. If they catch a wind, you can fly right into Mueller's lap."

When we got to the bay, Mueller was all set up at the beach house, the manual in his hands. Panic set in. "Will," I said, "did you study?"

He shrugged. "I started to, but something came up."

"Put your manuals away," Mueller said. "Denson, take attendance. From now on, anybody who is late more than three times is off the team. Understood?"

"Understood," everybody said.

Then he stood up and began walking around. "Okay. First question: Who can tell me the difference between a Lifesaver and a Lifeguard?"

Nobody raised a hand.

"Okay, we'll break it down. Denson, does a lifesaver react to an emergency or react to an accident?"

"An accident."

"That's right. A lifeguard acts to first prevent the accident and then does react to an emergency. A lifesaver reacts to an accident, acting after the fact. What's the difference, Bradford?"

I shrugged.

"Can a lifesaver be found liable and negligent in a court, Bradford?"

"I guess."

"Well, you guessed wrong," he said. "Let me ask you something else. Out of seventy-five hundred drownings that happen each year, how many occur around guarded areas?"

"Five hundred maybe."

"Try fifteen hundred. You'd better get your ass in gear and know this by Friday. 'Cause I'm testing you on it. Understand?"

I nodded.

"I asked you a question. Answer it."

"I understand."

"And take off that hat. It's enough to act like Gomer Pyle, you don't have to look like him, too."

"Look who's talking," Will whispered. "Sergeant Carter's seven-hundred-pound clone."

I took the hat off.

"Well," he said, almost smiling, "that's an improvement."

He drilled us for another hour. Treaded us for an hour. And ran us in the sand for a while.

When Mueller finally let us go, Aph and I wanted to go up to the Y, but Will was being a pain about it.

"When do we do the mowing?"

"We'll do it later this afternoon," I said. "I think I've figured something out."

"I don't want to hear it."

We couldn't talk him into going. He kept saying he had something to take care of. "But I'll bike up to the bridge with you guys."

As soon as we started out, I asked Aph what she thought of my hair.

"I told you. It's disgusting."

"And do you know how long it's going to take to grow back?" Will said.

I didn't answer him.

"Well, I'll tell you. By the end of the summer you might have three-quarters of an inch. If we had longer mornings, it'd grow faster. Hair grows fastest in the morning."

"Who cares?" I said.

"I do," Aphie said. "How do you know that, Will?"

"His grandmother," I said.

"Not my grandmother. It's a fact. And it picks up speed between four and six P.M. and then it slows down again. When you're sleeping it hardly grows at all."

If my mother heard that one, she'd have me up all night. I rubbed my hand over my head. "No more comments. Understand?"

"One more. This one *is* from my grandmother. They have this contest in that paper she reads. You send in a question and if they use it, you get a free subscription. The best one was about hair. If all the hair that grows on the body were to grow in a sort of hair cable, not individual hairs, how long would it grow in a year?"

"Is this a riddle?"

"No, Aph. It was in the paper and they backed it up with scientific data."

75

"Okay. Okay," I said, trying to shut him up. "How long?"

"By the end of the year, it would be thirty-seven miles long. Thirty-seven miles. That's from here to Manhattan almost."

Aph burst out laughing and so did I. I could just see one hair growing up from the top of my head, one lone hair, dying to get into Manhattan. So one day, I'm standing in my bedroom and the hair gets out the window, goes down the driveway, along Shore Road, and onto the Parkway. Then it hits the Expressway and goes through the tunnel and — bam — the hair is on Second Avenue heading downtown. And I'm still standing in my bedroom.

"Will, you're crazy," I said. "You're real crazy."

For the first time today, he smiled. Then he said maybe he'd see us up at the pool.

"Make it definite," I said. "You need the practice."

"Yeah, yeah, yeah, I need the practice."

"What does that mean?"

He didn't answer, and headed over the bridge. "See you later," he called back. "Maybe."

"Geez," I said, under my breath, "he is getting weird." And he was. He tells me how terrific Aph is, and how she's getting to look like the best-looking girl in town, and then he refuses to go up to the pool with her.

We had just about started up the road to the Y when Aphie stopped and hopped off her bike. "Answer me something," she said. "Why did you do it? Why all of a sudden is it so important to be like Denson and his crowd?"

I didn't answer.

"You never wanted to be like them before."

"Things change."

"What things?"

"A lot of things. And what's so bad about being like the rest of the guys?"

"What's so good about it?"

"A lot of things. Like not being called Curlers."

"So what was so bad about that?"

"Easy for you to say."

"Maybe when you get to like yourself enough to be yourself, you'll be able to say it, too."

She got back on her bike and pedaled up the hill.

"You mad or something?" I said.

She didn't answer me.

"I'm going to show Mueller," I said. "You'll see. I'm going to show everybody that Bradford is a winner."

"Fine," she called back. "But don't lose what you have."

"What do you mean by that?" I yelled, trying to catch up with her.

She didn't answer.

"Did you hear me?"

She still didn't answer, she just kept pedaling as though she were on a straightaway, leaving me far behind.

"You baffle me," I shouted. "You really do."

And she did.

11

"Mom, you've got to see me," I said when I got home from the Y. "You won't believe it."

She looked over at me. "I wish I didn't believe it, but I see it with my own eyes. And I don't like what I see."

"Not my hair, Mom. You've got to see me maneuver in the water. I'm getting good. Real good."

"Are you trying to tell me it's because you cut off that beautiful hair?" she said, as she put a chicken in the oven. "I won't buy that one."

"Well, it doesn't get in my eyes anymore."

"See if this is on three hundred fifty degrees, will you? I can't see the numbers without my glasses."

"It's okay," I said. "Did Will call?"

She nodded. "Said he'd call you later."

"Where'd he call from?"

"He didn't say." She took something out of the freezer. My mother freezes everything. Meat. Bread. Cookies. Pantyhose. My brother's wedding cake, and he's been married for three years. Esme's graduation cake from the Conservatory. My Cub Scout candy. My father's pancakes . . .

"Ted, are you listening to me?"

"What?"

"I said I have a new student coming in this afternoon. An older woman."

"If she's as old as Miss Sullivan, you should think of taking CPR," I said, scooping out some ice cream.

"That's not funny. And don't leave that ice cream out. Put it back in the freezer, and listen to me."

"I'm listening, Mom."

"Please try not to aggravate Esme. She's not in the best of moods."

"When is she?"

She looked over at me. "Ted, enough. Have some understanding. She's been away for almost four years. She's lonely."

"Better lonely than Richard."

"Much as I hate to admit it, I agree."

"Did you see him looking in the mirror all through dinner?"

She nodded. "Your father was so annoyed."

"What a jerk. And those flowers. They nearly asphyxiated me."

"Well, next time he invites himself, I'll know

better," she said. "But I do wish Esme would meet someone. So does your father." She sighed. "Oh, well, someday." She started toward the living room, then turned and said, "And remember what you promised about the guitar. From now until dinner. And no aggravating routines. Promise?"

"Let's eat early then. I've got mowing to do."

Sometimes I feel sorry for my mother. Teaching piano at home to a bunch of weirdos. She never says anything, but I think she does it just for the money. She's cheap, but only with certain things. I know she's helping Nathaniel. He's had it with feet and wants to go back to medical school. She should have been doing more than teaching piano. And my father should be doing more than selling building supplies. He should be building. It bothered me sometimes. They were old and getting older. I scooped out more ice cream and went upstairs.

"Don't tie up that phone," Esme called out. "I'm expecting a call."

"I'm just walking by the phone," I said. "And you're always waiting for a call."

She came out of her room and stood by the door. "You're right, Ted. And it never comes." She sort of sighed and went back to her room.

I really felt like a jerk when she said that. She was a pain, that was true, but she hadn't always been that way. "Hey, Esme," I said. "I'm sorry."

"It's okay. I guess I've got too much time on my hands."

That was true, too. The only thing she'd done since

she came back from Chicago was get on my back. And sit by the phone.

"Hey," I said, walking into her room, "I've got an idea. You want to do some mowing with Will and me? The pay is good."

She gave me one of her looks and said, "You have got to be kidding."

I shrugged. "Just trying to help." I started back to my room and bam, it came to me. Dan. Up at the Y. When Aph and I had seen him today, he had asked us if we typed. "I'll pay the going rate," he said. But Aphie didn't type, and neither did I.

"Hey, Esme, do you type?"

"I hate to type."

"But do you type?"

"Doesn't everybody?"

I told her about the job and what a great guy he was. "He's nice. Real nice. He lives with his uncle so he can work up at the Y for the summer. He doesn't know anybody in town because he's from Ohio. He's probably lonely. . . ."

"Nice try, Ted. But I am not looking for an Ohio version of Richard."

I tried to tell her that he wasn't like Richard, but she wouldn't listen. She said she'd find her own job. "And I'm not that desperate that my little brother has to ferret out a friend for me."

That was a matter of opinion.

I got my guitar out and practiced until dinnertime, but I couldn't get my fingers to do what I wanted. Krauss had given me two sheets of exercises and two pieces of music to have ready by tomorrow. He was a tough little guy and he scared me at times. He'd get into these little rages. Once he made me leave the room and told me to stand outside until I could get serious.

Everybody wanted me serious. Serious at fifteen? At twenty-five, maybe. But not now.

"Ted," Esme called, "it's Will."

I raced down the hall and grabbed the phone.

"Thank you," Esme said, in her snotty tone.

"Thank you, Esme," I said, bowing. "Thank you very much."

"Hey, Will, why didn't you want to come up to the pool?"

"I told you. I had something I had to do."

"Like what?"

"Like none of your business."

"What's with you? You need the practice just as much as I do. And besides, you've been telling me how terrific Aph is getting and you don't bother coming up."

He didn't answer.

"Will? Are you sore about the mowing? I told you I'd make it up."

No answer.

"Are you still there?"

"I'm still here, but I got to go."

"Where now?"

"Sozio came by to see my grandmother. He wants us to finish at least that pool area by tomorrow."

"I'll come over as soon as I finish dinner."

"If I'm not here, I'll leave the mower by the filter."

"Where will you be?" He didn't answer. "Oh, I guess this is your way of getting back at me, right?"

"See you tomorrow," he said, and he hung up.

I put the receiver down and sat back. "Cripes, he's getting to be a bigger nag than Esme."

12

Friday, the thirteenth of July, was the worst day of my life. The morning went fine. Practice at the beach was bearable. Even with Mueller and his bullhorn.

Smiddy asked him when we were going to get into the big stuff. "When do we get to save somebody?"

"Not until all you guys have enough practice in just plain old swimming. Remember, the course is six weeks long."

Even Will was acting more like himself. I'd mowed until dark last night. He wasn't around when I got there, but he showed up just as I was putting the mower away. "You got a lot done," he said. He was definitely pleased. He helped me put the rakes and stuff away and then we did a few laps in the pool. We didn't use the john before we went in and after we'd been in a while, Will had to go. Bad. "Geez," he said, "I'm not going to make it upstairs."

"So get out and piss. It's dark. Nobody will see you."

I swear he just about got started when every outdoor light in the place went on. The pool looked like Times Square. "Cripes," he said, taking off for the lobby door, "why do I listen to you?"

Mueller was still giving him a hard time. I kept telling him not to pay any attention. But Aph told me to mind my business. "Just because he's eased up on you doesn't give you the right to be handing out advice."

Mueller finally let us go at quarter to one. I turned to Will and said, "I've got to get to Krauss's by one. Then we'll mow. Want to meet me somewhere?"

"Where?"

"At Duke's?"

"Okay," he said. "You coming, Aph?"

"Can't. I promised my mother I'd straighten up the house for the weekend. We're expecting company."

It was a little after one when I got to Krauss's. He was waiting for me in his music room, sitting on the couch sipping something from a cup. "All ready, Theodore?"

I took my guitar out of its case.

"Now," he said, in his clipped accent. "Now we begin."

I nodded.

"The scales first, please."

My hands felt like claws; they just wouldn't do what

I wanted them to do. The scales were hard, but not beyond me. I could read them with no trouble, but my fingers were stiff.

"Lacks movement," he said. "Try it again."

I did.

"Again."

No better.

"Try the next one, if you would be so kind."

I hadn't even looked at the next one, but I started.

"Stop," he said. "It is terrible to try to play something one has no knowledge of, and it is worse to have to sit and listen to it. Have you practiced anything?"

"The two pieces." I had, but not much.

"Play the rondo, please. Do it slowly at first, if you would."

I was getting more nervous because Mr. Krauss got up and started to pace. He looked out the window and then began to pace again.

He finished pacing. "Stop," he said, putting his hands to his ears. "Please stop."

He came over to me. "Please be good enough to sit down."

I put my guitar down and sat on the couch.

"Do you know how many students I have?"

"I don't know."

"Twenty. I have twenty students."

He paced back and forth again.

"Do you know how many students of mine have talent?"

I shook my head.

His back was to me. "I asked you a question."

"I don't know."

"Guess."

"Fifteen."

"I have two. Two."

He turned and faced me. "And do you know who they are?"

"No, Mr. Krauss."

"Justine Weber is one. You are the other. The rest have little or no talent. But that is all right, because they know they don't. I know they don't. Their parents, who are paying for their lessons, know they don't. But they practice. Or they are out of here. And they do practice. And do you know what?"

I shook my head.

"They play better than you did today. They know where to put their fingers. Even if they cannot play with their hearts and their souls, they know where to put their fingers."

My stomach began to flip around.

"And you. You have the talent to know what it is to play with your heart and your soul, but do you know what to do with your fingers?"

I didn't answer him.

"I asked you a question. Please answer."

"I'm sorry."

"So am I," he said. "Do you know what it is like to teach music?"

"Yes," I said, "my mother teaches music."

"I didn't ask you what your mother does. I know what your mother does and that is one of the reasons I am so upset today."

"I'm sorry."

"You said that. And now I will tell you what it is like to teach other people music. Talented people. It is beautiful. It is like nothing else I have experienced. To impart what I know to somebody else. To see that person play what I have played myself. And when I discover somebody who is better at it than myself, that is a gift. You are better than I am. But you are the worst student I have."

"I'm sorry."

"If you say that one more time, I am going to lose what little patience I am trying to keep."

He went over to his desk, took something out, and handed it to me. "You give this back to your mother."

I looked down and saw it was the money I had given him for the lesson. "But I can't do that."

"And I cannot take your mother's good money any longer. I no longer want to be aggravated like this."

"Please, Mr. Krauss," I said, jumping up from the couch. "Please, I'll practice. I'll do anything. But please don't do this."

"I am sorry," he said. "Did you hear me? But I am not going to be used as a time waster by you."

Then I said something I lived to regret. "But I won't be able to stay on the swim team. If you cancel me out, I won't be able to take the lifeguard test."

He pounced on me. "Too bad. Tough two shoes. That is your problem. Not mine." He walked over to the couch and picked up my guitar. "You see," he said, "I am correct. You would rather swim to such a degree that you have lost your interest in music." He handed me my guitar. "So swim."

I begged him. I pleaded with him. But Mr. Krauss remained firm. "No more lessons to waste my time. And I will tell you something, Theodore. The day you can show me and yourself that you recognize your talent, that is the day I will listen. Till then, there's the door."

"I'll do it. You'll see. Can I come back next week?"

"Absolutely not."

"The next week?"

He shook his head. "Your intentions may be good, but it will not happen."

I put my guitar back in the case and headed toward the door, turning back one last time. "I'll be back," I said. "I will."

Mr. Krauss shook his head. "And one last thing," he said. "Your head looks as foolish outside as it is inside."

CHAPTER

13

When I got to Duke's, Will was waiting outside for me.

"You look awful," he said.

I felt awful. Terrified was more like it. What was I going to tell my mother? This would really do it. No practice. No lessons. No Krauss. No swimming. No lifeguard.

"What are you going to do?" Will said, after I told him what happened.

"I'm thinking."

Maybe Krauss wouldn't tell my mother. He never called her, and he lived on the other side of town. The chances of her running into him weren't great. But it could happen. Geez. It would happen. My mother was on some kind of committee down at the library, and she told me that Krauss was on it, too.

"I'm a dead man, Will."

90

"You look it. Your whole head is white," he said. "Come on, let's get going."

"I got to think. I've really got to think."

"It's a long way home. You can think on the way."

I tried to remember when the committee met. Maybe it was one of those things that only met once a month or so and didn't meet in the summer . . .

"It's starting to rain," Will said. "Move it."

. . . or maybe I could watch the mail for the notices that come from the library. . . .

"What's the matter with you?" Will yelled. "Let's head for cover."

I never realized how useful hair is, especially when it rains. It catches the rain before it gets to your face. Now that I had no hair, I had to keep wiping my eyes so I could see.

We headed for the overpass at Shore Road, walking our bikes down the hill. When we got settled, Will pulled out a couple of candy bars and handed me one. "This place comes in handy."

"I'm dead, Will."

"You said that."

"But I am."

He stuffed the candy bar in his mouth. "So what are you going to do about it?"

"Well, I'm not going to go home and tell her Krauss threw me out."

"So what are you going to tell her, that Krauss went on a world tour?"

"No," I said, "but I'll think of something."

"And you think you'll get away with it?"

"I don't need that."

"I'm being practical. Besides, it's a known fact . . ."

"You know what you can do with those facts?"

". . . statistics prove that unless you're a pathological liar, you'll get found out . . ."

"Cut it out."

". . . because the average person can't track a lie like a pathological liar can."

"Why?"

"Because the average person forgets the background of the lie."

"What are you talking about?"

"Let's say you tell your mother that Krauss went on a world tour. Then maybe two or three weeks later, your mom says something like, 'I wonder when Mr. Krauss will be back?' More than likely you'll say something like, 'From where?' "

"Why would I say that?"

"Because Krauss never went on a world tour, dummy," he said, smiling. "You made it up, and, like the average person, you're going to forget about the world tour because it never happened."

"Where'd you learn all this stuff?"

Will shrugged, the smile gone. "I've had a good teacher."

"What if I tell her nothing?" I said.

"What do you mean?"

"I just pretend I'm going to the lessons. I practice, and every Friday, I take my guitar and go."

"You'll never get away with it."

"Why?"

"Because something is going to trip you up."

"Will you stop all this negative stuff? I don't need it. I'm in trouble."

It was the only way out. She'd never understand. Between the lessons and my hair, she'd say I was really not individualizing and that'd be the end of my becoming a lifeguard.

"You'll be in more trouble. For one thing, what are you going to do with the money?"

"I'm not going to take it. I'm going to save it. I'll open a money-market fund, and when Krauss starts up the lessons again, I'll give it back." I looked over at Will. "Geez, Will, no matter what I do, I'm dead now or later."

He nodded. "Take it easy. Maybe Krauss will take you back."

"No. Not for a while anyway."

"And you can forget about a money-market fund. You need at least a hundred bucks to open one."

"Listen," I said, "don't tell anybody. Not your mother, or anybody. Not even Aph."

"What do you think I am? Some kind of creep who goes around telling things? You think I'd do that to you?"

I felt all crawly inside. I'm no George Washington, but I'm pretty truthful. And this was a lie. A big one. But what else was I going to do?

"I'll tell you one thing," I said. "Krauss is going to

take me back, because I'm going to practice till my fingers fall off."

"When?" Will said. "When do you do that? And when do we get the freaking mowing done?"

"I told you —"

"You're thinking. I know. But right now we don't have time to take a leak."

That was the truth. Maybe if I gave up sleeping. My hair would grow faster, too, but I'd probably be dead by the end of the summer. There was practice from seven thirty to noon at the beach, then practice at the pool, then mowing, then dinner, then dishes, then mowing, then sleep. And then there would be CPR.

"Maybe you should give up practicing at the pool."

"No way," I said. "Maybe we can do something about the mowing —"

"With what you promised?" Will said. "Remember that dumb card you gave Mr. Sozio: 'T AND W LAWN SERVICES IS AT YOUR SERVICE. NO JOB IS TOO BIG FOR T AND W. WE CARE.' And remember how Mr. Sozio had us sign a contract?"

"I'll think of something."

"If I hear that again, I'm going to puke," he said, reaching in his pocket for more candy and passing some to me.

"I've got to do it. Kind of lie, I mean. It's not like I want to do it, I've got no choice."

He shrugged. "Then you better keep it simple."

"What do you mean?"

"Like when she asks you something about Krauss,

you don't say, 'The lesson went great. Fantastic. Mr. Krauss said. . . .' You know what I mean."

"What do I say?"

"You say, fine, and let it go. Don't go into details because statistics prove that that's when liars get caught."

"Okay, so I say fine when she asks me. That's it?"

"That's it."

"What if she asks me something about Krauss?"

"Say he's fine, too. She's not going to ask him."

"But she might," I said, and then I told him about the committee. "I've got to find out when it meets."

"What are you going to say? 'Hey, Mom, I've been wondering when the Musicale Committee meets down at the library?' She'll think you've really flipped out."

"So what do I do?"

"Be cool. Call the library."

"What if they send those little cards in the mail telling her when it meets?"

"You ask when they send them out, then you camp at the mailbox."

"This doesn't seem simple."

"That's why I'm telling you to act cool."

"You ever lie, Will?"

He looked away for a minute. "Everybody tells little ones."

"I mean like this?"

He shrugged. "I probably would."

"Thanks, I needed that."

"Remember." He held out his hand to check on the

rain. "Don't get into complicated explanations. You're dead if you do."

"I'm probably going to be dead anyway," I said, tossing the candy wrapper at Will.

"We better get going," Will said, swatting it back at me. "It stopped raining. We can get some mowing done."

And all the way home, I kept telling myself things could be worse. I could be a pathological liar instead of an ordinary liar. With no guilt. I could tell my mother that Mr. Krauss moved back to Austria to take care of his ailing grandmother because he was the only family member she had left. I could make up stories to fit every occasion and remember them.

"See you as soon as you change," Will said, when we got to the top of his street. "And remember, keep it short and sweet."

When I got home, my mother called to me from the living room. "I'm in here, Ted. How was your lesson?"

"Fine."

"Was Mr. Krauss pleased?"

"Yes."

"Good," she said, "I'm glad."

It made me feel even worse when she said that. She trusted me. But what was I going to do? I had no choice. When I got up to my room, I took the money out of my pocket and hid it in an old sneaker in my closet. Then I changed my clothes and headed over to Will's to start mowing. And that's when the idea first came to me.

14

"It'll work, I tell you."

"You're crazy," Will said. "You're getting yourself in deeper."

"Be reasonable, Will. With another good power mower, we can mow twice as fast. It'll save us time." Time that I could spend with the guitar so I could get back to Krauss quicker and rid myself of all this guilt.

"Look at this," I said, pointing to what we had already mowed. "We've been mowing for three hours and we've still got all the back lawns to do. I tell you it's the only way to go."

But Will wouldn't budge. He was acting so weird. We argued the whole time we mowed. And about the craziest things. "You're cutting too close to the flowers. Didn't Sozio tell you not to go near them?"

"He also said to make sure the grass was clipped by the flowers. How am I supposed to do both?"

"That's your problem, big shot. You were the one who said, 'T and W Lawn Services enhances —' "

"Yeah, that's what I said. T and W Lawn Services enhances the beauty of your grounds. T and W Lawn Services aims for perfection. T and W employs only the finest craftsmen."

He used to break up when I did that routine, but this time he didn't even smile. And when we started to clip in front of his apartment and his grandmother kept calling out to him, he told her to shut up. Under his breath.

"Hey," I said, "what's the matter, Will? You're acting strange. You got a problem or something?"

"No. No problem."

"You're sore at me about something, aren't you?" And before he could answer, I said, "It's the mowing, I know it. But I'm going to solve that."

"Will you shut the hell up about it, and just mow."

But I didn't shut up, I kept at it. I figured if we put a down payment on another mower and on an electric clipper at the second-hand mower shop, we could pay the balance with the salary Sozio paid us. Without them, we'd be mowing lawns till midnight every night and we still wouldn't get through all we had to do.

On Monday morning at practice, just after Mueller told Aph and Steve Howe to get in the water so he could clock them, Will finally broke down. "Okay, okay. I'll do it."

"Great," I said, standing up so I could see what was

going on with Aph and Steve. She pulled out ahead of Steve a second after they hit the water. She was good and getting better. But so was I. Mueller told me it was the haircut, but it was more than that. My kick had been getting better ever since I got the fins. The first couple of days I used them, I could barely walk when I got out of the pool. But they worked. Will used them once. Said they'd destroyed his arches for life. I swear he's sabotaging himself.

"Are you listening?" Will said.

"To what?"

"I said I'm not signing my name to any loan. No way. No how. No signature on any —"

"Who asked you to?"

Aphie ran over to us, dripping wet, leaned over toward Will and me, and shook her head. "That'll cool you off."

She looked over at me. "What are you two arguing about now?" She flopped down on the blanket.

"No argument," I said. "Business discussion. We need more tools." And before I could tell her how great she'd looked in the water, Mueller called out, "Smiddy. Denson. Bradford. Report to the boat."

I couldn't believe it, Mueller was teaming me up with Denson. Smiddy, okay. But Denson. It was always just Will and me.

I looked down at Will. He gave me a funny smile and said, "You're moving up in the world."

"Yeah. Sure." I threw down my towel, stepped over Will, and ran down to where Mueller was standing. He was calling out instructions to the kids who were in the water. "You people swim over to the buoy and then come on out." Then he turned to us and said, "You three do the same as they're doing when you get in. I'm starting practice testing today. Real testing starts on Friday."

I knew what that meant. Mueller had told us that if anyone didn't pass the preliminary testing, they couldn't go on for the actual lifeguard course.

I said a quick prayer, and when the other kids got out, I headed for the water and waited for Mueller to give us the go-ahead. I remembered what Dan had told me about holding my head close to the water and concentrating. Shut out everything and everybody. But it was hard. I could hear the other kids hollering back and forth and Mueller was ordering everybody on the beach to do some leg exercises.

"Okay," Mueller said to us, "get ready. When I count to three, get started. And remember, this is only a practice. So don't tighten up. Especially you, Bradford. You'll do better."

I couldn't believe he'd said that to me. He sounded almost human. When he yelled, "Three," I took off. I tried to keep my head close to the water, but every once in a while, I'd look up to see where Denson and Smiddy were. And then I'd lose time. "Concentrate," I said out loud. "Forget about them." When I got to the buoy, I could see that Denson and Smiddy were heading back already. That really threw me. I put my head close in and started back.

"Good work, Denson. You, too, Smiddy." Then

Mueller looked over at me and said, "Not bad, Bradford. Like I said, you'll do better if you don't tighten up. Get up on the beach and run for five." Then he called the rest of the kids. When I passed Will, I wished him luck.

I ran in the sand for more than five, and all the while I could hear Mueller giving the kids instructions. It seemed like every other name was Loughlin.

"Hey, Bradford," Denson said when I ran by him, "your friend's not doing so good."

"He'll be okay. He just needs practice."

"He needs more than practice."

I kept running, and when I circled around and came back toward him, Denson stood up. "Hey, when is enough enough?" he said. "Let's go get a Coke."

"No thanks," I said.

"Aaah, come on," he said. "Mueller's busy with his bullhorn. He won't miss us."

He put his arm around me and headed me toward The Shack. "You're doing real good, buddy boy. You getting private lessons or something?"

"Not really," I said, "but I've been going up to the Y."

"You're taking lessons with that faggot, Capra?"

"He's no faggot," I said. "Anyway, he's given me some good tips."

"You want tips?" he said, putting his hand on my shoulder. "You're looking at the guy who can give them. And not just swimming tips. You get my drift?"

I didn't answer.

"Hey, there, Debbie girl," Denson said when we got to a group of girls sitting near The Shack. "Long time, no see."

"I've been here every day," she said.

"Way to go, Debs." He bent down, gave her cheek a quick squeeze and said, "Catch you later."

He put his arm around me again and leaned toward me. "She wants my body. Every girl I meet wants my body. You got that problem?"

I shrugged.

"Hey, give it time. And I guarantee if you keep going the way you're going, it'll happen. Soon." He turned and gave me his Stallone smile. "You ever get laid?"

I didn't answer. What was I going to tell him? That up until last year, I thought only chickens did that?

"Let me tell you, buddy, it beats anything." He moved closer and said, "I hear Mary Beth thinks you're getting to be a pretty cool guy." He looked around like there was somebody spying on us, then eyeballed me and said, "You want to try it sometime?"

I shrugged again. But, geez, Mary Beth. Just thinking about it made me look down to check myself out.

"Well, if you ever do, let me know."

"Th-thanks," I said.

"It'll be my pleasure." He nudged me hard. "And yours."

At The Shack, he bought two Cokes and we stood drinking them. Between gulps he told me he could pass the survival test with his hands tied and that he'd ace the written test. "No sweat." He was so sure of himself. He felt like I wanted to feel. It made me think about what Mueller had said a few days ago. "Stick with the winners. The drive they have rubs off."

"Come on," he said, "let's go where the action is." He walked over to where the girls sat, me following. Lori Stephens jumped up and ran over to him. "Hi, Ray," she said. "Can I have a sip?" He handed her his Coke.

"Anything for a pal," he said. He winked at me. "Anything. Right, Bradford?"

I nodded. God, I hope my face didn't look as hot as it felt.

"Hey, Ted," Debbie said, "you're doing great. You make Will look pathetic."

I shrugged and laughed a tiny little laugh. Lori handed Ray his Coke and walked over to me. She smiled up at me and poked my belly button. My face felt like it was on fire.

"That's not hard to do with Will," she said, still smiling up at me.

I shrugged again, not saying anything, which made me feel kind of lousy. But what could I say?

"Are you the strong, silent type?" she said, reaching up to pat my head. She came up to my Adam's apple and she was definitely not one of those girls who carried a violin case with the bow on the outside. She took my Coke out of my hand. "I'm still awfully thirsty, Teddy. Do you mind?"

I shook my head.

"Hey," Denson yelled. "Watch this." And for no reason I could figure out, he did a handstand and started walking around on his hands. He made his way over to where Debbie was sitting, and, when he got there, he flipped over and stretched out at her feet.

"Silly," she said, bending over to kiss him.

"I was thirsty," Lori said, tossing my empty can on the sand. "I drank up all your Coke." Then she reached over and snapped the elastic on my bathing suit. "You *are* the strong, silent type."

My face was on fire for sure now. "I . . . I . . . better go," I said. "Um, um, I got things to do."

"See you," she said. "But tomorrow, I treat."

"Ooooeee," Denson said. "Better watch it, Bradford." Then he curled up beside Debbie and pulled at her bathing suit strap.

I started back toward where Aphie was sitting in the sand, waiting for Will. Geez, what was that all about? Lori Stephens trying to make out with me. She had this reputation for being kind of tough. "Just her exterior," Aphie once said. "She's really a good person." But I didn't know her interior and she kind of scared me. Now, Mary Beth was different. Something like Aph, not so much in looks and definitely not as serious as Aph, but there was something.

Will was still in the water when I got to where Aph was. I could hear Mueller bellowing something about everybody's timing being off by minutes, not seconds. And when I heard "Loughlin" for the forty-ninth time, my stomach tightened.

I stretched out beside Aphie. She was picking up sand and letting it sift through her fingers.

I pulled at the towel she had around her shoulders.

"Stop it," she said.

"Excuse me, Madame," I said, putting her towel back around her shoulders.

"Don't be cute. You don't have to be. It's me you're talking to."

"What do you mean by that?"

"Forget it," she said, picking up more sand. "It's not important." She held her hand up high, made a fist, and let the sand fall slowly down. Then she turned to me. "But there *is* something important. Will. There's definitely something going on with him."

"You're telling me?" I said. "Yesterday he was fine, but when I went over to mow, he was one big pain in the butt. He told me I was his problem."

"Maybe it's all this stupid tension. So he's not a lifeguard. What's the big deal about it anyway?"

"I'll tell you what's the big deal about being a lifeguard. It proves something."

"What?"

"It proves that I'm as good as the next guy."

"And Will won't be if he doesn't make it?"

"I didn't say that. But I'll bet he won't feel good about himself."

Aphie got up. "That's your opinion," she said and started toward the shore.

"Hey, wait," I said, "I'll go with you."

But she kept going and I had to run to catch up with her.

"You sore?"

"Would it matter?"

I shrugged and kept walking. But when I thought about it, it would.

"Yeah," I said. "It would matter."

Then she started up again. Telling me how ridiculous it was to try to be like everybody else, telling me how silly it was for me to have cut off all my hair.

Then she stopped walking. "How do you think Will felt when you got to go in with Ray? Or did that occur to you?"

"It wasn't my idea," I said. "I'm not the coach. Besides, Aph, I am getting better than Will."

"Qualify that. Better at swimming. Nothing else."

"Come on, Aph. . . ."

She looked at me for a long minute, shook her head and said, "I'm going down to meet Will."

Then she turned and ran toward the water.

15

"I don't need this aggravation," Will said when he and Aphie walked by me. "I've got enough aggravation in my life."

I followed them back to where we had our things. "You did okay," I said. "You made the timing."

"Who cares?"

"You do. I do. We all do."

He looked over at me. "Speak for yourself. I mean it. I don't give a flying —"

"*Watch* your language."

"Sorry, Aphie. I'm sorry. Really." Then he turned and headed toward The Shack. "I'm thirsty," he said.

I went after him and when he got something to drink, I asked him for a swallow. I took a short one, handed the can back to him, and said, "Something's bugging you."

He shook his head.

"If it's the mowing, Will, I've got that under control. From today on —"

"Right now, I don't give a crap about the mowing."

"What?" I said. "You've been bitching about it ever since we started."

He put the can up to his lips and drank.

"If it's not the mowing, what is it?"

He kept drinking.

"Hey, Will," I said, "it wasn't my idea to go in with Denson and Smiddy. . . ."

"I don't give a crap about them either." He looked down at the can, made a fist, and crushed it. "I've had it."

I started to say something, but he stopped me cold. "I'm quitting, and I don't want to talk about it. To anybody. Understood?"

"What about Aph?"

"Especially Aph."

"Hey, if it's because of the mowing, we'll have more time now. We'll finish it off —"

"I told you, Ted, I don't want to talk about it."

"You sure it's got nothing to do with what Mueller did?"

He nodded and aimed the can for a trash barrel. It missed. And without bothering to pick it up, he headed back to the blanket.

I felt lousy about Will's quitting, not so much that he'd done it, but the way it made me feel. Kind of relieved.

Aph had dressed and was drying her hair when we got back. "I've got to go," she said. "I've got a dentist appointment."

"You mean you're not going to the Y?"

She shrugged. "Maybe later." She looked over at Will. "You okay?"

"Fine," he said.

"You sure?"

"Sure," he said. "See you tomorrow."

Mueller started to bellow through his bullhorn again, and when he was through, Will and I headed downtown to Burns Mower Shop. I miscalculated the amount of money it would take to get a power mower and clipper. "Eighty-five dollars," Mr. Burns said. "Can't go any lower. Take it or leave it."

Will wanted to leave it, but I told Mr. Burns we'd take it. I figured I'd use the money Krauss had given back to me and with that, plus $15 of my own money and $15 of Will's, it'd make $50. I signed an IOU for $35 and told Mr. Burns we'd pick up the mower and clipper before five o'clock.

"Doors close at five sharp," he said.

"We'll be here," I said.

I tried to get Will to go up to the Y, but he wouldn't.

"I've got things to do," he said.

"What things? I told you the mowing's going to be a breeze with what we have now. We'll mow after dinner."

But he still wouldn't budge.

I headed up to the pool. I couldn't remember the

last time I had biked anywhere without Will. Or Aph. It felt strange. I felt a little guilty that I was going alone. And since I was already on a guilt trip, I thought about all the lies that were building up. Cripes, I could spend the rest of my life feeling guilty.

As soon as I got to the pool, I knew I wasn't going to get any serious practice in. Denson was there with what looked like his whole crowd. Somebody had a radio blaring and Denson was fooling around with Denise Doherty at the far end of the pool.

"Hey, Bradford," he said. "Glad you mentioned this. Water's great." He winked at me. "Lori's waiting."

"Got to shower first," I said.

"Do you believe him?" he said to Denise.

"It's the rule."

"Rules suck," I heard him say, as I headed toward the locker room.

I took a fast shower, and as I got out and reached for my towel, I heard a girl's voice. I jumped back, yanked the curtain in place, and waited.

"Stop it. I told you, not here."

It was Mary Beth Atwood.

"Where then?"

With Smiddy.

"I don't know. But not here."

"You putting me on?"

She said something that I couldn't hear. I didn't know whether to start up the shower again or just stand there shivering. I took a quick look from behind the curtain and when I did, I saw them. Not all of them. Just their feet. They were in the first-aid stall with the curtain drawn.

"This is gross," I heard Mary Beth say. "Let's go back in the pool."

"You had no intention of doing anything," Jerry said, his voice cutting. "You were just putting me on."

"You should talk about putting people on," she said.

"What do you mean by that?"

"You and Lori?"

He laughed. "You got to be kidding. Me? With her?"

"That's what Betsy told me."

"Betsy Dealy? What does she know? She's like a nun, for cripessake. She and Aph would make a good pair. And speaking of pairs, that's one of the reasons Lori doesn't turn me on. Her headlights are so big they belong on a Mack truck."

"Oh. My. God," Mary Beth said. "You *are* a rat. That's not what Lori told Betsy. . . ."

"Screw Betsy."

Smack!

"What the . . ."

"You're disgusting," Mary Beth said. "Let me out of here."

There was a scuffle and then it sounded like somebody fell.

"What do you think you're doing?" Smiddy said. "Cut it out."

The next thing I knew, I heard bare feet running across the floor, and then a second later, heavier footsteps.

"Wait a minute," Smiddy called after her. "You got me all wrong. . . ."

I stood there. Naked. Shivering. Wishing I were an umbrella so I could just fold up. Geez, Mary Beth and Smiddy. And Smiddy and Lori. I yanked on my suit, grabbed my towel, and headed back to the pool.

Mary Beth wasn't there. But the rest of them were. The music was loud and when I looked around for Smiddy, he was in the pool. With Lori Stephens. I swear it was weird. They were holding hands and he was swishing her back and forth the way my father used to do to us when we were kids. Denson and Denise were stretched out on a mat. Debbie and a few of the others were doing a line dance around the pool. It was like a zoo.

"Want to dance?" Debbie called over.

"I think I'll do a few laps first."

"Come on, Teddio," she said. "You've been doing that all morning."

"Later," I said. "Thanks anyway."

I swam the length of the pool underwater. When I surfaced, I caught a glimpse of Denson making out with Denise. I looked the other way, and when I did, I saw Smiddy head toward the locker room. And the next thing I knew, Lori was swimming next to me. I pretended I didn't notice her and kept swimming. So did she. She was pretty good. Almost as good as Aph. Geez, this is all I need. More pressure. To be beaten by Denson is one thing, but if Aph and Lori beat me out, I'd have to leave town.

After about five laps, and when we hit the low end of the pool, she reached out and said, "You want that treat now?"

I swear I thought I'd die.

I stood up and so did she. "Well," she said, "are you ready?"

"I . . . promised Will I'd . . ."

"Coke or orange? Diet or regular?" she asked, smiling. "Or milk?"

I felt like a real idiot. "Coke," I said. "Diet."

"You coming or not?" Smiddy called from the locker room. "I'm ready to head out."

"Be with you in a sec," she said, leaning over toward me. "I'll give you a rain check. See you at the beach."

"Yeah," I said, "see you at the beach."

The music was getting louder, and Denson was still making out with Denise. I started to swim, trying to shut them out. I practiced my kick and made sure my head was close to the water. I forced myself not to look at anybody. After a while I started to time myself. I watched the clock on the wall and kind of amazed myself. I was doing better than I thought. I could make it back and forth in the pool in less than three minutes. Then two.

"Knock it off, you guys," I heard somebody yell. "Can't you read the signs? No running." It was Dan.

"We're dancing," Debbie said.

"I don't care what you call it, quit it."

"Hey," Denson said, "relax, Mr. C. We're splitting."

He yelled over to Debbie and everybody started to pack up. "Come on, Bradford. It's splitsville."

"You with these guys?" Dan said, looking over at me.

I shrugged. "I guess."

"You coming, Bradford?"

"I think I'll put in a little more time," I said.

"Okay by me, pal."

"See you tomorrow."

"Not if I see you first," Denson said, smiling his best Stallone smile.

When he got out of earshot, Dan asked, "Is that the rest of the team?"

"Not all of them."

"It's enough," he said. He looked down at me. "How's your timing? Any better?"

"Two minutes and about ten seconds a complete lap."

"Terrific. Want me to check it?"

"Sure," I said, looking up at the clock, and when I saw the time, I hauled myself out of the pool. Fast. It was almost four-thirty. Burns's closed at five and Will would kill me if I didn't mow tonight. I headed toward the phone. "I've got to call home," I said. "I'll be right back."

"I'm going to do a pool check. Let me know when you want me to time you."

I dialed and when Esme picked up the phone, I asked her to pick me up.

"I can't," she said. "I just highlighted my hair. I'm a mess."

"Nobody will see you. Please, Esme. It's a matter of life and death. Mine."

"Well, if that's all it is," she said, "forget it."

"Esme," I yelled. "Please. I'm desperate."

"I've got to go. The color is running down my face."

"Esme. Don't. I need a ride." But she hung up.

"I'll give you a lift," Dan called over. "Just give me a couple of minutes."

After I picked the mower and stuff up at Burns's, we couldn't fit my bike back into the trunk. I gave Dan directions to the house and said I'd meet him there. On the way home, I decided to get back at Esme. When I got there, Dan was waiting in the driveway. After we got everything out of the trunk, I said, "You still need somebody to type?"

He nodded. "You know someone?"

"My sister."

"Did you ask her?"

I nodded.

"She'll do it?"

"No problem. Why don't you come in and I'll introduce you?"

"You sure it's all right?"

I set him up in the kitchen with some lemonade. I checked around to see what my mother was up to. Then I remembered. She and my father had gone into New York for their annual dinner and play. Talk about luck.

I headed upstairs. "Be right back," I called to Dan.

115

"Hey, Esme," I yelled. "Where are you?"

She opened the bathroom door. I swear she looked like a witch. She had a plastic shower cap on and her face looked jaundiced.

"It's the highlighter," she said. "What do you want?"

"You better come down and check out the smell in the kitchen."

"What smell?"

"I don't know. But it smells awful."

"Are you sure? I was just down there. I didn't smell anything."

"Okay. But don't blame me if the kitchen explodes. It smells like gas."

She sighed and pulled her robe tighter. "Oh, God," she said. "I'll never get through this summer."

I ran down ahead of her and waited. She pushed the kitchen door open and looked around. "What smell are you talking . . ."

"Esme," I said, "this is Dan. Dan this is Esme."

"How — how — how do you do," Dan said, his eyes wide. He stood up fast, so fast his foot hit the chairrail. The chair crashed down. "I'm sorry," he said, reaching down to pick it up. "My feet sometimes do these things." He slid the chair under the table, smiled a goofy smile, and said, "It'll be safer there." Then he turned back to Esme and said, "I want to thank you for agreeing to take the job."

"What job?"

"The typing job. Ted said you —"

"Will you excuse us, please?" she said in a little tight

116

voice. She turned and faced me, her eyes glaring. She took my arm and yanked me into the dining room.

"You little rat," she whispered. "How could you?"

And before I could answer, she said, "I'm going upstairs and if I'm up there ten minutes or ten hours, don't you dare leave this house. You hear me?"

"I've got to get over to Will's. I've got to mow."

"I'll mow you, if you leave before I look human," she hissed through her teeth. "How could you let anybody see me like this?" She ran up the stairs, but stopped before she got to the top. "And fix him another lemonade."

The rest is history.

Life is not easy. One day you get up and everything is fine. The next day everything stinks. And it's all got to do with the people in your life. I swear it does.

Take Esme, for instance. That part of my life isn't bad. She almost demolished me the night I brought Dan home, but now it's fine. She's been almost nice. For a while I thought I created a monster, because for about two days she didn't do anything but type. But then she found out Dan was a music major at Ohio Wesleyan. "Fate brought us together," she said. She's got a lousy memory, too.

Things are okay with Mueller. And Denson's still being real friendly. But ever since the day at the pool, I feel as though I've got to be on my guard with him and his crowd. Especially the girls. I never feel that way when I'm hanging out with Aph. At least I never did, and I don't really now, but even she's getting to me. She keeps telling me how I should get to the bottom of what's bothering Will. And when she found out Will had quit the team, she all but quit, too.

And Will. He's really driving me nuts. He's changed so much since the end of school, he's like a different guy. I'm getting tired of wondering what's going on with him. "If it's not the mowing, and it's not the swimming, what is it?" I keep asking him.

He said maybe it was his allergies.

"That's bull," I said.

And the other day, I knew for sure it was bull. The two of us were mowing the pool area. I was running around with the mower and Will was using the electric clipper to prune some bushes. His grandmother came out and said he had a telephone call. He dropped the clipper, raced across the grass, and disappeared for about a week. *And* he left the clipper on and destroyed an azalea bush.

When he came back out and I asked him what it was all about, he first told me to butt out. But I kept pushing. And I never push. "I'm getting sick of this. Who was that on the phone?"

"My father," he said.

I kept quiet.

Will sees his father once in a while, but he doesn't talk about him much. In fact, he hardly has talked about him since that time when we were eleven. His dad had flown in from somewhere for Will's birthday. He told Will he could do anything he wanted that day. Anything. Go anywhere. And he could take anybody along with him. "Take your whole class," his father had said. But Will just asked me.

I can still feel that day. We went to Shea Stadium to see the Mets play the Reds. We weren't there for two minutes when his father got up and told us he was going for hot dogs. He was gone so long, we kept taking turns going to the hot dog stands looking for him. It was awful. But it was worse when he came back, because he had this lady hanging on his arm. She looked about a thousand and she had red hair that looked like it was starched. And if I live to be as old as that lady, I'll never forget what she said. "Oh, my gawd, Max," she said, pointing her finger at me, "he's the spittin' image of you." And his father didn't tell her it was Will who was his son. He just stood there smiling.

I don't remember who won the game that day. When it was over, Will's dad gave us money for train fare. "I've got to take Lucille on home," he'd said. But I do remember Will on that train ride home. He didn't say one word. Not one word. And when we got to the station and he'd called his mother to pick us up, he turned to me and said, "I'm telling her it was okay. Okay?" I said, "Okay," and we never talked about it again.

"You want to talk about it?" I said.

He didn't answer.

"Okay. If that's the way you want it," I said. "You want to go to Duke's for lunch? I'll treat."

No answer.

"Come on, you'll never get me in such a generous mood again," I said, hoping he'd say yes.

He looked over at me and I swear I thought he was going to bust out crying. I didn't want to see him do that, so I grabbed the mower and shut the motor off. Then I got the clipper. "Boy," I said, holding up the clipper, "we're going to catch it from Sozio. It's alive. It ate the azalea."

After a while, Will said, "You still want to go to Duke's?"

"Sure," I said, fishing into my pocket to see if I had enough money.

After I put the tools away we got our bikes and headed for town. We didn't say much; Will kind of tagged behind me. I was thinking of all the things I could say to get him in a better mood.

I slowed down so we could ride side by side.

Just before we got to town, Will stopped pedaling and pulled over to the side of the road. He walked his bike over the tracks and through the eelgrass. I followed. When the bay was visible, he sat down. I sat beside him.

We didn't talk for a while and then Will said in almost a whisper, "He wants me to come for a visit. A long one."

"Where?"

"He's in Manhattan now, but he wants me to go out to Seattle with him."

"What's in Seattle?"

"He's got a new job."

I didn't say anything. He always had a new job.

"You going?"

"I don't know."

He kept pulling up dandelions and blowing on them, scattering the seeds everywhere.

"Hey," I said, "Mr. Sozio would kick your butt if he saw you doing that. 'I break your head you make more weeds,' he'd say."

But Will didn't laugh. He didn't even smile.

"Would you go if you were me?" he said.

I shrugged. But what I wanted to say was there was no way I'd go visit that creep. Even for a day. And then I thought of something else. If Will went, what was I supposed to do about the mowing? Thinking like that made me feel like a number one rat.

"He sounds different," Will said. "Real up."

Up to what? I wanted to say, but all I said was, "When would you go?"

"Few days, maybe."

"He's got reservations?"

"He said we'd go by bus."

"Who's we?"

"Just us, I guess."

"It'll take you a year to get there."

Will kept making dandelions.

"Does your mom know about this?"

He shook his head.

"What about your grandmother?"

He nodded.

"What does she say?"

He shrugged. "She's confused. She still can't believe he left us. And she can't believe he's been into all the stuff he's been into."

He stretched out and closed his eyes. I stretched out beside him. "He's been calling you for a while now, hasn't he?"

He nodded.

"You been seeing him?"

He nodded again.

"That's what the allergies were all about."

We didn't say anything after that. After a long time, Will turned to me. "I asked Justine Weber's brother if he'd take on the mowing."

"So you are going."

He sat up, and, as seriously as I ever heard Will sound in my life, said, "Sometimes you don't have a choice." He stretched out again. "He sounded different. He really wants me. Can you believe it?"

I wanted to grab him and say, "Are you crazy? Of course I don't believe it." But instead I said, "People change. Look at Esme."

"Yeah," he said, "they do."

"When are you going to tell your mom?"

"Tomorrow. The next day. She'll understand. She's never really put him down in front of me. She told me once that maybe his problems started in Vietnam. But you know what?"

And before I could answer, he said, "My grandmother, his own mother, says that's not true. As much as she doesn't want to believe he's screwed up, even she says it wasn't that. She told me he was secretary to some hotshot officer. He never really was in the war."

We stayed there, stretched out in the grass. It was long and swayed over our faces. We didn't talk, but I swear I could hear what Will was thinking. And I felt guilty for not having the guts to tell him how I really felt. And I felt guiltier for thinking about how this was going to really screw up my summer.

Guilt. It's my middle name.

CHAPTER

17

Ever since Will decided to go to Seattle, my life has been a series of complications. He told me not to say anything to anybody about anything, so I haven't. And because of that, Aphie keeps telling me what a creep I am. "He's your best friend. Find out what's bothering him." When I told her it was none of my business, she said, "You're impossible. Can't you think of anything else but that stupid swimming? You've changed. And not for the better."

I keep telling her that I haven't changed, that sometimes life takes you in different directions, but it doesn't mean that you're heading in that direction forever. She told me to shut up.

But the biggest complication happened this morning. When practice was over down at the bay, I raced back to Will's to finish up the lawn around the pool area. Will was there clipping the back lawn. I mowed as fast as I could, hoping to get in some real practicing up at the Y. When Will finished, he yelled over, "Want a Coke?"

"Make it cold," I yelled back. I finished up by the pool and decided to clip around the garage. A car pulled into the driveway. Our car. And my father was driving it.

"Hey, Dad," I yelled. "What are you doing here?"

"Just driving by." He motioned for me to come over and when I got to the car, he said, "Do you know what today is?"

"It's . . ." And then I remembered. It was Friday.

Will was right. You've got to be a pathological liar to keep a lie going. I had forgotten all about Krauss.

"I'll wait till you're finished," he said. "Then we'll go for a burger."

My heart pumped faster. I pushed the mower back to the pool house. Will met me halfway.

"Here," he said, handing me a Coke. "It's cold."

"I don't want it. My father is waiting out front."

"So?"

"So, I'm supposed to be at Krauss's."

"Oh, geez."

I shoved the mower into the pool house and started back. Will ran after me. "Be calm. Just tell him the facts. He'll understand."

"Sure. Sure, he'll understand."

My father didn't say one word to me when I got into the car, and all the way to Casey's he didn't say anything. He had the radio on and he tapped his fingers on the wheel and kind of hummed along.

When we got settled at Casey's, he said, "I'm hungry. I'm going for the platter."

"Sounds good," I said, even though I knew I couldn't eat.

He still didn't say anything, and the longer he didn't speak, the worse it was.

"Mom teaching?"

He nodded. "Pauline and Miss Sullivan were sitting on the porch when I left. Seems one of them is there at the wrong time."

The burgers came, and Dad ate his slowly. He picked up one french fry after another, dipping each one into the ketchup, looking at it before taking large bites. "I wish your mother could master french fries. But you can't be good at everything, can you, Ted?"

It was a little question, but it was a big question. I knew he didn't expect me to say that my mother was good at a lot of things, but couldn't make french fries. He wanted me to start telling him what was happening. But Will had said to keep it simple. "No," I said, "you can't."

He finished his burger and ordered more coffee. "So, tell me, son, what's up?"

"What do you mean?" I said, stalling for time.

"I ran into Mr. Krauss this morning at the library."

I kind of nodded with my whole body. "How is he?"

"Fine."

When he said that I knew I was doomed. "He told you, didn't he?"

He nodded slowly and said, "But I want you to tell me in your own words."

The waitress came over with more coffee and my father asked for apple pie with ice cream. I didn't want any.

"It's not what you think."

"You mean Mr. Krauss just imagines that you're no longer taking lessons from him?"

"No. I mean it's not what you think. I'm not just taking the money and keeping it."

"I should hope not."

"I've got it all saved. Except for what I spent on the mower and the clipper. And I'm going to take care of that."

"Ted," he said, leaning over toward me, "you can be sure I'll get to the money issue. But now, tell me what happened."

"You mean he didn't tell you?"

He shook his head. "Your own words, please."

"Dad," I said, "he threw me out. He wouldn't let me come back."

"I gathered that."

When I got through with the whole story, I asked him if he was going to tell my mother.

"Do we ever keep things from one another?"

"But this will mean I'll be out of the running for lifeguard."

"Why didn't you think of that before?"

"I did. But it just happened. I tried. I really tried. I

told Krauss. I promised him. I told him I'd practice ninety hours a week, but he wouldn't listen."

"And have you been practicing?"

"I have."

"I haven't heard you doing much."

I was dead and I knew it.

"I have practiced, but not enough. I don't have the time, Dad. I'm swimming down at the bay. And then I swim up at the Y. And then Will and I mow."

"But you made a deal."

"I know I did, but it got kind of impossible."

"Then why didn't you try to renegotiate? Maybe take lessons every other week. Your mother isn't unreasonable."

That was his opinion, not mine. "Please don't tell her." I leaned forward and said, "This means a lot to me, Dad. I'm good now. You should see me. I'm beating most of the kids in the time workouts. I've got to do it. I'll die if I can't."

"I doubt that."

But I *would* die. Some part of me would die. The part that was thinking I could do anything.

"Please, Dad?" I felt like crying and I hated myself for that. I took a deep breath and waited for the feeling to pass and then I said again, "Please. I'll never ask for another thing."

He sighed and ran his hand through his hair. Then he looked straight at me for a long while. The waitress came and filled his cup with more coffee and brought his apple pie and ice cream, but he didn't touch it. He just kept looking over at me.

"I put the money in the bank, Dad. I wasn't going to use it, just for the mower and the clipper, and I'm paying it back."

He shook his head. "No excuses, Ted. No excuse excuses a lie."

"I didn't want to lie. Ask Will. But if I told Mom, that would have been the end of it right then and there."

"I can't agree with that."

"It's true."

"In your opinion."

He paid the bill and the two of us walked out toward the car. "Mr. Krauss said you were his best student."

"But I'm good at other things, too. You'll see. . . ."

He stopped walking and put his arm around me and just looked at me. After a long time, he nodded and half smiled, then told me to get into the car.

He put the key in the ignition and pumped the gas pedal, but he didn't start the motor. He sighed. And then he sighed again.

"Ted," he said, looking over at me, "I'm going to tell you something I haven't thought of in a long, long while."

He leaned back and looked out the side window.

"I was fifteen once," he said softly, "and I thought I knew everything." He looked back at me. "But life taught me otherwise."

I started to say something, but he put his finger to his lips and said, "Wait, now. Please. Let me finish."

I nodded.

"And it's been my best teacher."

Then he looked straight ahead and said, "Maybe it's time for you to begin learning that way. To find out just what it is that you want."

"You mean you're not going to tell Mom?"

"Not just yet," he said. "And maybe I won't tell her at all." Then he looked at me, his gaze steady, his voice low. "Because one day you will. And you know, Ted, I think that day might come sooner than you imagine right now."

CHAPTER

18

Sometimes friendship can be one pain in the tail. When it came time for Will to tell his mom he had been seeing his father and that he was going out to Seattle with him, he talked me into coming over for dinner. "This way, she won't get all crazy. She likes you, and you can tell her things will be okay."

But I knew things wouldn't be okay. My own life was certainly not okay. I was beginning to get freaked out about the testing. And if I wasn't freaking out about that, it was the mowing. And Esme. She *had* changed. For about a week. Then she started driving me crazy again. "Do you realize it's only three weeks till Mom and Dad's anniversary?" she said yesterday. And when I told her there was only a week to go before Mueller started to hold the qualifying tests, she said that was my problem.

"You haven't given me one penny toward the party." This was true.

"And you promised you'd help me with all the rest of it, and you haven't done one thing."

That was true, too.

And then there was my mother. It was really getting to me, her not knowing about Krauss. Every time I came back from what was supposed to be a lesson, or every time she heard me playing the guitar, she'd say something that piled more guilt on. Like, "You're sounding better every day." Or, "Mr. Krauss must be so pleased." And the one that really got to me. "My goodness, take it easy. I heard the guitar at midnight. You've got to get your rest. That big swimming test is coming up soon."

To tell the truth, playing the guitar kind of relaxed me. It was the only time I wasn't chasing my tail. Until Esme told me we couldn't afford to pay the trio she'd tried to get for the party and that I'd have to provide the music. "Will can play the drums," she said, "and Dan said he can fill in on the piano." When I tried to tell her Will probably wouldn't be around, she told me I'd have to figure that problem out for myself. And when I asked her where I was supposed to find the time to learn all the old futzy fifties music she wanted me to play, she told me that was my problem, too.

Will's mom almost lost it the night Will told her he was going. I swear if emotions generated hydrogen, the Wexford Arms would have been a memory.

"You're doing what?" his mom said, as she sat down at the dinner table.

"I'm visiting Dad," Will said, passing me the potatoes. I passed them to Will's grandmother. She dropped them.

"It's the vapors," Marietta said, jumping up and fanning Will's grandmother with her napkin.

"Sit down, Marietta," Will's mom said. "Now." She looked over at his grandmother. "Stop it, Mother. No dramatics. Do you hear me?"

"She can't help it," Marietta said.

"Yes, she can," Will's mother said, "and she knows it as well as I do."

I felt kind of sorry for his grandmother. It was sad looking at her. And sadder to hear her. "He's not a bad boy, Beth. Just a bit mixed up."

"Mother. Please. Not now." Then she turned to Will. "How long has this been going on? Why didn't he call me? How dare he plan something like this with you."

"I'm going, Mom," Will said quietly.

Mrs. Loughlin got up and headed toward her bedroom. "We'll see about that."

"What are you going to do?"

"I'm calling him." She slammed her bedroom door.

Will got up from the table and banged on her door. "Mom," he yelled, "I'm going. You're not going to stop me." He waited for a minute. "You hear me? I'm going. I'm not a little kid."

After a while, Will's mom came out. She looked as though she'd been crying.

Will reached out and put his hand on her arm and said, "I've got a right to see him, Mom. He's my father."

She stood still, shaking her head back and forth. Then she put her hand on Will's, took a deep breath and said, "Clear up, why don't you? I'll put dessert out in a while."

I felt crawly being there listening to it all, so I got up and helped Will in the kitchen. But even in there I could hear them. "You'll see, Beth," Will's grandmother said, "the boys will have a fine time."

"Max is not a boy, Mother, and I don't give a damn about him. It's Will I'm concerned about. I don't want you raising his hopes. You know your son. And I know Max."

When Will's mom finally came into the kitchen, she didn't say too much. She told Will they'd have to go shopping for some new clothes and asked if he needed new sneakers. "You know how Max likes everything just so." And then she told me she'd take me home after we had dessert. "I've got things to do downtown."

She really didn't have to go downtown; I knew that the minute I got in the car. "Sometimes I wish I could take off," she said, her hands clutching the steering wheel. "Dear God, how did I get stuck with all of this?"

She reached out and gave my hand a quick squeeze. "Sorry, Ted. I didn't offer to drive you home so you could hear me carry on like this."

"It's okay." But I was glad she had stopped because

I had enough stuff to deal with. One part of me felt sorry for Will but another part of me wanted to deck him. He kept saying it was my idea about the mowing and that was true, but he was no innocent victim. And here he was going off to Seattle, getting me sucked into his mess and not giving a thought to how he was screwing me up.

She started the motor. "Shall I go down Shore Road or go through town?"

"Shore Road's easier," I said.

"Will's going to be hurt," she said, as she turned into my street. "Max will see to that."

"Maybe Mr. Loughlin has changed."

"He is *not* the type of person who is blessed by miracles."

When we got to my house, she turned the motor off and we sat there for a while. "I've always been glad you and Will are friends." She laughed a little. "Even though the two of you can be royal pains." She turned to me. "Keep in touch with him. He's going to need you." Then she kissed me quickly on the cheek and started up the motor.

I got out and stood at the curb, watching the car go down the street. Then I turned and started up the walk. The light in my father's den was on. He probably was in there looking over some house plans, like he always did. I climbed the porch steps, opened the screen door, and when I passed the den, there he was. And for some crazy reason, I almost wanted to go in and kiss him. But I just said good-night.

Will called me real early the next morning. He told

me his plans had changed and his father was going to pick him up early Sunday morning. "Come over early and stay over tonight," he said. "Everybody's getting crazy over here."

He was waiting for me in the lobby when I got there. "Sozio wants us to clip around the pool before we do anything else."

"Cripes," I said. "I swear, if I could find a way to put a broom in each ear and one up —"

"Knock it off. My grandmother's getting off the elevator."

"Where's she going?"

"She's been. I told you she wants to be the next Mrs. Sozio."

We clipped the pool area and then decided to take a quick swim. We did some laps and when the air turned cold, we sneaked into the sauna. We dropped our bathing suits on the floor and stretched out on towels.

The dry, hot air felt good.

"If my grandmother saw us, she'd probably tell us she read about a guy who shriveled up in one of these."

"I can just see the headline," I said. "Two five-foot-ten, no, make that one five-foot-ten and one five-foot-eleven — I grew an inch — young men go into Wexford Arms Sauna and come out seven inches high."

"And it goes on to say, 'The Big Apple Circus signs them up for their road show,' " Will said.

"But they refuse to go."

"Why?"

"Because one seven-inch schmuck quit and is going to Seattle." I sat up and looked over at Will. "You could have gone all the way."

"What do you mean?"

"Swimming. Lifeguard. Remember?"

"You think so?" He turned over on his stomach. "For cripessake, it was almost killing me."

"The swimming or Mueller?"

"Maybe a little of both. Let's face it, most of the other kids are better."

"That's your opinion."

"It's the truth. And you know what? It's not so bad."

"What do you mean, it's not so bad?"

"Because I decided I don't really need it. I know I'm no jock. Everybody else knows that, too. But it's okay."

"You're really not sorry?"

He shook his head. "Nope." He got up and wrapped his towel around him and headed for the door. "Let's get out of here. I think I just lost an inch."

Will's dad didn't show up on Sunday morning. Nobody said anything about it. It was just like any morning. Will's mom made us breakfast and Marietta looked for Loretta on TV. Will's grandmother sat out on the terrace where she could watch for cars pulling into the driveway. Aph called to say she was on her way over to say good-bye, but Will told her he probably wasn't going anywhere.

When Will and I finished breakfast, I said we should

go out to do some mowing. "It'll get your mind off this," I said. "And it'll get Sozio off my back for a while."

Lunch came and went. Will's mom brought us cold drinks at about four and just as she put the tray down by the pool, Will's grandmother called him from the terrace. "Hurry up, Will," she said, waving the phone. "Here he is."

Will ran over and took the phone. Will's mom walked over slowly. Will kept nodding his head and even though I couldn't hear what he was saying, I knew he didn't like what he was hearing. When he handed the telephone back to his grandmother, he turned to his mother.

"The Port Authority?" Will's mom said in a loud voice. "Is he crazy?"

She turned to me and said, "Did you hear that? He's sending a taxi for him." Then she turned to Will and said, "You're not going."

I didn't want to hear it all again, but it would have been rude to leave. Will said something about his promising to meet his father at eight by the information booth.

"Eight o'clock on a Sunday night?" she said. "He expects you to meet him alone at that place at eight o'clock?"

Will nodded.

"Well, you're not going to do it. Do you hear me? I'm not going to let you do it." She looked like she was going to cry. "He may not even show up."

"Mom," Will said, "he will."

There was so much confusion after that, I didn't know where to go. Will's grandmother kept saying how lucky Will was at his age to be taking a trip cross-country. "You'll see things you've never seen before."

"I'll just bet he will," Will's mom said. "Before he leaves the bus station."

She turned to Will's grandmother. "Tell him. Tell him how many times you've read about young people disappearing from there. . . ."

"Oh, now, Beth," she said. "You can't believe all you read."

Things got crazier. Will kept saying he was going and nobody was going to stop him. "It'll be okay."

"Over my dead body you'll go with . . ." Will's mom stopped talking and sat down. She kept taking deep breaths and after a while, she looked up at Will and said, "Maybe it's time you learn for yourself."

Will didn't say anything.

"But you're not meeting him alone. I'll drive you in."

I wanted to go, too, but Mrs. Loughlin said she was going to call her sister in Manhattan. "I'll ask her if I can spend the night." She looked over at Will. "I think Will and I should take this trip alone."

She got up and put her arm around him. "Why don't you go get your things? We'll stop somewhere for a bite to eat. It will make the waiting easier."

I headed back to where I'd left the mower, glad to be away from it all. "Geez," I said under my breath. "That guy is crazy."

When the time came for Will to leave, he came

down to where I was mowing. He had on new jeans and his mother had treated him to a new sport coat.

Will must have called Aphie because she came running into the courtyard.

"You look great," she said, kissing him on the cheek. "And don't forget to write."

Will beamed. "Every day."

I told him not to get fresh with the ladies on the bus and to call me. "You can call collect. Okay?"

"Still acting like Mr. Big Shot," he said, smiling.

"Come on, Will," Mrs. Loughlin said, "we'd better get going."

Aph stood and waved until the car got out of the driveway, then she turned to me and said, "Didn't he look great?"

I shrugged and pushed the mower toward the pool house.

"What's the matter?" she said, following behind me.

"You owe me an apology."

"Why?"

"For all the things you said about me being a lousy friend."

"Oh, that. Well, you should have told me."

"And rat on Will?"

"Okay," she said. "For that, I'm sorry, but . . ."

"I knew there was a 'but' coming."

". . . I still say it's dumb to try to be like everybody else," she said. "You want to know something else?"

And before I could answer she said, "You were okay the way you were."

CHAPTER

19

To be honest, things down at practice are better without Will around. I don't feel so pressured. And I'm doing great. Mueller says my timing is just where it should be. "Your kick is strong," he said to me this morning. And when I told him I'd been practicing with fins, he got his bullhorn out and said, "From now on, I want you guys to practice with weights on your legs."

He turned to me. "Where'd you get them?"

"Ashford's."

"You can get fins at Ashford's. Share them if Ashford runs out."

Denson came over and asked me if he could borrow mine.

"Okay if I use them here?" he said. "The Y is definitely not my style."

He hadn't been up to the Y since that day, and neither had anybody else. Except me and Aph.

Lori Stephens is still going around with Smiddy — a fact I can't figure out. And Denson does a disappearing act with Debbie every time Mueller turns around. Mary Beth hasn't been around lately.

Everything else is falling apart. I mean really falling apart. This morning, Justine's brother told me he wouldn't be able to mow anymore, and Mr. Sozio is going to put my tail in a sling before the summer is over.

And Esme. It was a mistake for me to get Dan Capra and my sister together. Now every time I'm up at the Y and he's not helping me with my backstroke, he's bugging me about how I should be practicing the music for the party.

The other day, Esme dragged him into the city and they brought home all this old fifties music that Esme tells me I have to learn for the party. "What do you think I am?" I keep asking her. "Five people?" But does she care that tomorrow is the big test that will make me eligible for the even bigger test? And I've still got the whole north section of Wexford Arms to mow? By myself.

And then there's my head. It looks awful. The hair that's growing back isn't like the hair I used to have. It sticks out like picks. I'm a mess. I try not to think about it, but even if I don't, there's always somebody there to remind me. Like just before I got into the shower tonight, my father said I reminded him of a Christmas gift he got as a kid. "It was a clay head. I think it was called a Gilly. I'd water it and grass grew all over its head. It was quite amazing."

When I got out of the shower, I decided to call Will to tell him about Justine's brother. I was really ticked off. Here he was out in Seattle having a great old time. Telling me all he was doing with his dad. Telling me how terrific things were. Never once asking me how things were going here. And calling me whenever he felt like it. Like the other morning, he called at two. "Do you know what time it is, Will?" I heard my father ask him. And when I got on the phone, he didn't even say he was sorry for waking up the whole house.

I dialed his father's number, and, as usual, got the answering machine. Even the answering machine ticked me off. "Hello, there," his father's voice said. "Congratulations for having called the right number at the wrong time. . . ." I hung up.

I was less than twelve hours away from the qualifying test with pressure from Mueller, pressure from Sozio, and pressure from Esme. I felt panicked. I got into bed and pulled my guitar out and started to play. It calmed me down and let me think straight. I was just getting into some James Taylor when the phone rang.

"Ted, it's me. Aphie. Justine told me her brother quit on you."

"He was doing a lousy job anyway."

"Do you need help?"

"Do I need help? Do the Eskimos need fur hats?"

"Who are you going to ask?"

"I've asked a million guys. Nobody's interested."

"You didn't ask me."

"You'd do it? You mean it?"

"Sure I mean it. When do I start?"

"Tomorrow. After the timing. And thanks."

"You coming by for me?"

"Sure."

"See you."

Boy, she surprises me at times. She's been on my back about Will since he left. "Did you call him?" "How's he doing?" "Tell him I said hi." "Give him my love." And now, she offers to save my life, for cripessake.

I played for a while and just as I was about to put the guitar away, it came to me. She's doing this for Will. Not me. She wants to make it okay for him. Geez, women are something.

I got into bed, but I had trouble falling asleep, and when I did, I kept waking up. In a cold sweat. What if I didn't pass the timing? My whole summer would have been a waste. I knew for sure Denson would pass. Aphie, too. I remembered what Dan had said when he talked at school that day. "Experience says only eighteen people make the qualifying timing." Eighteen from the whole county. I had to be one of them. At first I did it almost out of spite. To show Denson. To let the girls know I was alive. But now, it was more than that. I want to show everybody that I can do anything. Anything. That nobody can stop me . . .

"Ted," I heard my mother say. "Ted. Wake up. It's after eight."

I opened my eyes and she was standing over me.

"Eight? Why didn't you wake me up? I was supposed to be there by eight."

"I thought you'd left. I would have called . . ."

I jumped out of bed, grabbed my bathing suit, and headed for the bathroom.

"Esme," I yelled when I went by her room. "Drive me! I'm late. . . ."

"Esme drove Dad to the yard," my mother said. "His car is in the shop."

"Oh, geez," I said. "Oh, geez."

"Watch your language."

"Do me a favor, please. Call Aphie and tell her it's too late for me to come by." Then I bolted for the bathroom and slammed the door.

I was out in two seconds and on my bike.

My mother ran out of the kitchen and called, "Good luck, Ted."

It was misty and when I got to Shore Road a fog was rolling in. By the time I got to the bay, it was really heavy. I could barely see Mueller's boat. Finally I spotted it, and Mueller spotted me. "You're late, Bradford. Run for ten, swim for ten, then you're on."

I ran for ten and then I walked toward the water. It was smooth and the fog was lifting just a little. I dived in. My body did exactly what I wanted it to do. I skimmed across the water, kicking my feet like there was a tiny outboard attached to them. I kept my head low the way Dan showed me, turning in the trough behind the bow wave to breathe. I glided across the top of the bay. Smooth. Fast. Sure of myself.

146

"That's it," Mueller boomed. "Denson. Smiddy. Bradford. Let's get set for the real thing."

I floated to shore and toweled myself dry to warm up. I was breathing hard. I stood there watching Denson get ready. And Smiddy. Denson did some knee bends and started to fool around with a few of the girls who had come down to wish him luck.

Then they came over to me. I felt good about that, even though I almost puked when Denise said, "Good luck, Teddikins."

I looked for Aphie, but she wasn't around. Lori Stephens was standing with Smiddy. She yelled over to me. "Hey, Ted, diet or regular when you qualify? My treat."

"Regular," I yelled back. "I'll splurge."

Mueller started up his usual recitation of how bay swimming was the only way to test a swimmer's strength. He went on about how this was just a preliminary to the real thing. "This is where we separate the boys from the future lifeguards," he said.

"Remember," he bellowed, "I'll be at least twenty feet in front of you. And when I've reached the two-hundred-meter marker, I stop. You've got exactly four minutes and twenty seconds to make it. Take your marks by the shore and when I blow the whistle, go for it."

When Mueller started to row out, I paced back and forth, my head down, my stomach jumping around. I jogged in place, moving every part of me, shaking my hands, wiggling my fingers.

"Ted. Ted." It was Aphie. She ran down toward me, but just before she got to me, Mueller let go with the whistle. I said a quick prayer and took off.

Mueller kept yelling orders, but I kept a steady pace, knowing I had to reserve my strength for the final push. I concentrated, really concentrated. Denson and Smiddy were ahead of me. I tried to block out Mueller's voice and the sound of their splashing. Don't worry, I kept telling myself. Keep it smooth. Nice and smooth. Keep your breathing smooth. I didn't lift my head out of the water much. Just a little. Concentrate. Concentrate. Don't blow it.

Don't lose it. Keep it smooth. They were about ten feet ahead of me. I still kept my pace. No hurry. Just keep it steady. Just a few more feet. Now. Now. Now. And I made my move. Still smooth. I kept my pace nice and steady, but faster. Mueller yelled. I kept gaining.

"Get moving, Bradford."

Concentrate. Shut him out. Don't listen. Keep your head down. Don't lose it now. Don't let me lose it. Please, God. And then I passed them. I kept going and when I got to the marker, I went around it and swam over to Mueller's boat. He grabbed my arm and pulled me in beside him. Then he reached down and pulled Denson into the boat. "You made it," he said, "by two seconds." And by the time Smiddy reached the boat, he'd lost it by twelve seconds. A lousy twelve seconds.

I was exhausted. My legs ached and my arms weighed about a thousand pounds. I'd swallowed some water and my head was pounding. But I felt great. I don't think in my whole life I ever felt that great. I beat Denson. Wait till Will heard that. Better time than Denson. And when we got back to shore, Debbie Harris ran up to me first. "You were marvelous," she said. Denson kind of shrugged, but I knew he felt like crap about that.

Lori bought me a regular Coke and gave me a kiss. Smiddy told her to cut it out.

Mueller even came over and put his arm around me. I wanted to pull away, but I didn't. "Good job, Bradford. Damn good job." Then he picked up his bullhorn and said, "The rest of you get down here by eight tomorrow morning. No exceptions."

Aphie was standing off by herself and when I went over to her, she smiled and congratulated me. "How about that? I beat Denson."

"I saw," she said. "And that's not all I saw, Mr. Big Shot. Now when do we start mowing?"

"What's with you, Aph? I just beat Denson, and all you can say is 'When do we mow?'?"

She shrugged.

"Maybe if Will had done it, it'd be a different story," I said.

"You are so dense."

"What do you mean by that?"

She shook her head. "Samson's strength disappeared with his hair. Your brains took off with yours."

She picked up her things. "Let's mow."

Geez, maybe if I live to be a thousand, I'll understand her. But I'm not counting on it.

20

My mother baked a cake the day I passed the qualifying time race. "Congratulations, Ted," it said in big
red letters. And it wasn't bad. It wasn't good. But it
wasn't bad.

Aphie passed the next day, but you'd never know it.
She beat out Steve Howe and Marty Reddy, but it was
as though she had beat them in a bathtub race. "Don't
you dare," she said to me when I tried to lift her on
my shoulders. "It's no big deal."

I'd tried to call Will to tell him I'd qualified, but
every time I did, I'd get that dumb answering machine.
And this morning when I spoke to Aphie, she told me
he'd called her. "What did he say when he heard I
qualified?"

"Not much."

"What'd he say when you told him you did?"

"He wasn't very talkative."

"Wait till I get him. He calls me at two in the morning to tell me what a great time he's having, and he doesn't even call to congratulate me or to wish me luck on the big one before the big, big one."

"I've got to go," Aphie said. "I'm late for church."

She was getting to be a bigger pain than Will. I swear if I flew from the top of the Empire State Building to Radio City Music Hall, she wouldn't react. I put the phone down and dialed out to Seattle again. The phone rang about a hundred times, then there were a couple of clicks, and just as I was going to hang up, Will's father answered.

"Hello, Mr. Loughlin," I said. "This is Ted. Is Will there?"

"Yo, there, sport," he said. "How are you?"

He sounded so phony, I wanted to puke. "I'm fine," I said.

"We're just fine out here, too," he said. "Busy. But having ourselves some good times . . ."

"That's nice. Can I talk to —"

"Wait up, sport, the other line is ringing."

He put me on hold, and I really felt like puking. Elevator music started. After about ninety-five songs, he got back on and said, "Sorry, Ted, that was my agent. Seems Paris needs my type of photography."

"Please, Mr. Loughlin," I said, remembering the hard time my mother had just given me over last month's phone bill, "can I talk to Will?"

"Sure thing, sport. I'll get him right now." And he put me on hold again.

About a thousand songs later, Will got on.

151

"Where were you?" I said.

"Outside."

"Where outside? Hawaii?"

"Ha. Ha."

"So what's new?"

"Nothing."

"When are you coming home?"

"I don't know."

"You're having a blast out there," I said. "And I'm working my butt off back here."

"You've got help."

"Some help. I swear Justine's brother quit before you got out of Manhattan. . . ."

"I didn't mean that help."

"Oh, you mean Aphie," I said. "Hey, what'd you think of us qualifying? And can you believe I beat Denson?"

"Hooray."

"What did you say?"

"I said, hoo-ray."

"What are you saying it like that for?"

He didn't answer me.

"Everything okay with you?"

"Fine," he said. "Just fine."

"It doesn't sound it." I didn't know whether to push or not. "How are you and your dad doing?"

"I told you. Things are fine."

"What's the matter then?"

He didn't answer.

"Will? You there?"

"I'm here."

"You mean things haven't changed."

"Who says that? I told you things are fine," he said, his voice rising. "You want to know something? You're the one who's changed. And you want to know something else? I'm sick of hearing about your damn swimming and your timing and that freakin' Denson. . . ." And then he told me he was pissed about my moving in on Aphie the minute he was out of sight.

"Hey, wait a minute, Will, she's just helping —"

"You're a damn liar. You know that? A damn liar."

I tried to get him to stop. I even tried to make him laugh, telling him I paid for the call.

"What, am I supposed to be grateful that the biggest jock in Bayview called?"

"Will —"

"Shut up."

"Hey, wait a minute, Will. Remember me? Ted? Buddy and friend —"

"Friend?" he hollered. "Friend? Who are you kidding? All you can think of is your damned self. You're probably sucking up to Mueller and kissing Denson's ass by now. . . ."

"Hey, Will," I yelled into the phone. "Knock it off. What's the matter with you?"

"Me? Nothing's the matter with me, Jocko. Nothing at all."

And he slammed down the phone.

I stood there looking at the phone. My legs started to shake. I dialed the number again, but after three rings, and the damn clicks, the voice on the answering machine said, "Hey, there, whoever you are, thanks for calling, but Max Loughlin has departed for parts —"

I slammed down the receiver and just looked at the phone.

Esme came out of her room. "What was that all about?"

"Nothing," I said.

"Nothing?"

"I don't want to talk about it."

"Okay. Okay," she said.

I went into my room and fell across the bed. I couldn't believe it. I didn't move in on Aph. No way. She asked if she could help. What'd he expect me to do? Tell her to buzz off? Saying all those lousy things. Calling me Jocko . . .

The phone rang. I leaped up and opened the door. Esme was coming out of her room.

"It's for me," I said, heading for the phone. "It's Will. . . ."

But she got to the phone before me. "Hello." She looked over at me, shook her head and said, "Hi, Dan."

My legs were still shaking and I felt like I was going to lose it. I went back to my room, slammed the door, and picked up my pillow and beat on it until the feathers floated around the room like dandelion seeds.

21

"Ted?" Esme said, knocking on the door. "Are you okay?"

I didn't want to answer her. I felt like somebody had hit me in the stomach with a baseball bat. How could he talk to me like that?

"Ted. Answer me."

He's jealous. All that talk about his not caring. That was bull. He's jealous I made it and he didn't.

"Ted, if you don't answer me, I'm coming in."

I should call him back and tell him what I —

"Ted. Open the door."

I went over and opened the door and then went back and stretched out on my bed.

"What's going on with you and Will?"

"Nothing."

"It didn't sound like nothing, and from the way you look. . . ."

"I don't want to talk about it."

"Well, if you do, I'll be around." She started toward the door.

"He called me a liar," I said.

She turned around. "Why?"

I shrugged. "It didn't even sound like Will. He sounded crazy."

"Maybe he's having a rough time. . . ."

"So am I," I yelled, and turned toward the wall.

"You don't have to scream. And if you want my opinion, you've brought your rough times on yourself."

I jumped up and faced her. "What are you talking about?"

"Nobody's pressuring you to do all you're doing."

"What? You're the one who told me I had to fork over money for the party. How am I supposed to do that if I don't do the mowing? And you're the one who told me I had to provide the music for the party so I'm practicing. . . ."

"You've always done those things."

"Oh," I said, "it's the swimming. You're like everybody else. It's the swimming that's making everybody crazy. Mom. Dad. You. Aph. And now Will."

"That's ridiculous."

"And you know why it makes everybody crazy? Because I'm doing something I *want* to do. Something I'm good at. And everybody else is doing stuff they *have* to do. Not because they want to."

"What are you talking about?"

"Look at Dad. You think he's happy at the lumberyard?" Before she could answer, I said, "He's not. And look at Mom. . . ."

"What about Mom?"

I didn't answer her.

"I asked you a question. Answer me."

"You think she's happy giving lessons to all those weirdos?"

"Yes. And as far as Dad is concerned —"

"I don't want to talk anymore," I said, getting back into bed and pulling the spread over my head. "I mean it. I don't want to talk."

"Doing that won't make it go away, Ted." And then in a very soft voice she said, "No one can stay under the covers long enough to do that."

The door closed and she was gone.

I couldn't stay still. I kept thinking about Will.

I got up and changed into a pair of jeans, stuffed my swimming gear in my bike pack and started downstairs. "Mom," I called, "I'll be back in a while."

"If you're going to mow, put a hat on. Your head will be scorched by the time you finish. And remember, dinner at four today."

I should have been mowing, but I needed to talk to somebody. My chest was tight and sore, like I'd been treading water for a hundred hours. I was going to bust open if I didn't talk to somebody. I headed up to the Y, hoping Dan would be there. He wasn't, so I started back home.

"Do you want to get killed?" somebody yelled. "Get out of the road!"

I straightened out my wheel and rode on the bike

157

path. I kept going until I got to Will's. It was quiet, like Sunday mornings always are, and hot. The grass was dry and the pool was still and deserted. Nobody was anywhere. I went into the pool house, changed into my suit, pushed the mower out, and started it up. The sun was so hot I tried to wrap my shirt around my head, but it kept falling off. I put it around my waist and started to mow. I kept at it until the grass around the pool was cut. Then I headed for the back area. . . .

"TED. TED. ARE YOU ALL RIGHT?"

". . . keep going. Keep it up. . . ."

"What are you talking about? Answer me."

My head felt like somebody was sitting on it, and when I could finally get my eyes open, I saw Aphie leaning over me.

"What happened? Are you okay?"

"I was mow —"

"I think you fainted. I'll get you water. Don't move. I'll be right back."

When she got back, Will's mother was with her. "Oh, my God," Mrs. Loughlin said. "What happened?"

She came over and the two of them helped me up. "I'm okay," I said.

They sat me down. "You need to drink something," Mrs. Loughlin said. "You're probably dehydrated."

"I'm okay," I said.

"Did you eat today?"

I shook my head. "What time is it?"

"Almost two," she said, putting a straw into a glass and holding it to my mouth.

I'd been here since eleven.

"Come on, Ted, drink this slowly." She turned to Aphie and said, "Would you go in and get an orange? And a banana . . ."

Aphie ran toward the lobby.

"And bring more Gatorade . . . and a blanket." She reached down and got my shirt and put it around me. "You're shivering. Are you cold?"

I nodded. "I feel so stupid," I said.

"It's the heat. Just relax. You'll be fine."

When Aphie got back, she put the blanket around me.

"It's a good thing you came over, Aphie," Mrs. Loughlin said, taking the orange from her hand and giving me a piece at a time. "Slowly now. And relax."

After a while, Mr. Sozio came out and offered to take me home. "How many times I got to tell you my son says to wear a hat? He's a big specialist. You got to wear a hat in the sun." He smiled at me. "Especially if you got no hair."

Mrs. Loughlin thanked him and said she'd take me home. She told me to wait while she got her keys, and when I asked her what to do with my bike, Aphie said she'd ride it home. "Then maybe Mrs. Loughlin can drive me back to get mine."

Mrs. Loughlin said that would be fine. Aphie stood over me, peeled the banana, and handed me half. "You scared me, Ted." Her eyes were watery. "I thought you were dead when I came into the courtyard and saw you lying there."

"Would you care?"

"What a stupid question." She turned away.

"Aph? You mad again?"

She looked straight at me. "How can you be so, so . . ." Then she looked around and said, "I'll come back when it cools down and finish up."

"Don't. We can do it tomorrow."

"I'll put the stuff away then."

"Stay," I said, holding out my hand.

She took it and then her face got all screwed up, but she didn't cry. "You dope," she said.

"Thanks, Aph."

"I didn't mean that," she said.

"And I wasn't being sarcastic," I said. "I meant thanks for being here."

She smiled and squeezed my hand. "That's okay. We're friends." She blew her nose.

Mrs. Loughlin came back with her keys, and even though I kept telling her I was fine, she helped me to her car. "See you later, Aph," I said.

She nodded. "See you."

When we got to my street, I asked Mrs. Loughlin if she'd pull the car over.

"You feeling sick to your stomach?"

"No," I said. "I just want to talk to you."

"What is it?"

"I heard from Will."

"You sound so serious. What is it?"

"He didn't sound good," I said, "but when I asked him if everything was okay, he said things were great."

"I doubt it. What else did he say?"

"He said he was sick of hearing about the swimming and just about everything else I was doing —"

"That's not like Will."

"— and then he accused me of moving in on Aph. I swear, Mrs. Loughlin, Aph's been on my back since he left. There's no way I could have moved in on her even if I'd wanted to." I looked away.

"Ted, none of this has anything to do with you. He was lashing out. You know that."

I shrugged. "But maybe a little bit of it is true," I said.

"Like what?"

"The swimming. But I didn't move in on Aph. I swear up until today, I thought she'd like me to disappear. And I have definitely not kissed Denson's ass — excuse me, Mrs. Loughlin, I'm really sorry."

"It's all right. And I'm sure you haven't." She put her hand on my arm. "Ted, you're entitled to do what you're doing. Just like Will. Do you understand?"

I shrugged again.

"He's hurting. I know that." She looked down at the dashboard. "His father and I aren't divorced. Did you know that?"

I shook my head.

"Max would never cooperate. He doesn't know how to let things go. He wants to hold on even though what he's holding on to doesn't mean too much to him." She took a deep breath. "And Will and I don't

161

mean too much to him. Nobody does. Not for long anyway."

"Maybe things have changed. . . ."

She shook her head. "You know better and so do I. And so does Will. But until Will sees that his father is not capable of being a father, much less the father he needs, he'll keep hoping against hope."

She turned the key. "I've got to get you home now."

We drove slowly down the street, not talking, and when we got to my house, she put her hand on mine and said, "I've told you this before, and I'm going to tell you again. I'm grateful that you and Will are friends. I always will be."

Then she helped me into the house and when she told my mother what had happened, my mother insisted that Dad take me to the doctor. The answering service couldn't find the doctor, so my mother had my father take me to the emergency room.

"Nothing wrong with this guy but the heat," the doctor said to my father. "Take him home and keep him quiet for a couple of days. He'll be fine."

When I tried to argue with the doctor about all I had to do, he just said, "That's tough. And if you weren't in such good shape physically, I'd keep you quiet for another day." Then he looked at my father. "Quiet. For two days." Then he looked at me and said, "Next time, wear a hat."

CHAPTER

22

If I ever faint again I'm going to make sure my mother is out of town. She hasn't left me alone for two minutes.

"How are you feeling?"

"Do you feel dizzy?"

"Is your stomach sick?"

"Keep your feet elevated."

"Hugh, drop the shade down, the sun is on his feet."

"Does your head ache?"

"Don't move from this porch."

"Are you thirsty?"

"Remember what the doctor said."

"Are you hungry?"

When she said that, my father looked over at me and winked. "You're not up to cooking, Emily. We'll get takeout at Casey's." He came over to where my mother had set me up. "You look like a balding Camille," he said, sitting down at the end of the glider.

"Hugh," my mother said, "don't sit there. The movement may make him dizzy."

"He's fine, Em," he said, leaning over to feel my forehead. "You too warm out here?"

"I'm fine."

"What can I get you? Chicken okay?"

"Anything."

"If it's on the menu, it's yours." Then he got up and said, "Come on, Em, take a drive with me."

"And leave him alone?"

He pointed to the driveway. "He'll be okay. Here's the baby-sitter." He waved. "Hey there, Aphie, just in time."

After my mother asked me another thousand questions, and after she told Aphie fifty times that they'd be right back, she started down the porch steps, but turned and said, "Aphie, if Esme calls, tell her to bring Dan over for some chicken."

My father winked at her. "Make sure you tell her it's from Casey's."

Aphie pulled a chair over and sat down. "How are you feeling?" she said. "What can I get you?"

"Geez," I said, "one leaves and another one comes."

"Are you telling me I sound like your mother?"

"Just like her."

She stuck her tongue out. "Does your mother do that, too?"

"All the time."

She laughed and said, "You're nuts."

164

"You want to hear some Taylor?" And when she said yes, I started to get up.

"You're not supposed to move. I'll get it."

We sat there, not talking, listening to the music, and when James Taylor started to sing, "Things may always stay the way they are . . . still my head looks for a change from time to time . . . ," I almost lost it.

"You okay?"

I nodded. "Do me a favor? Hand me the phone through the window. I'm going to try Will." Then I realized I hadn't told her about my last phone conversation with Will, so I did. Everything except what he said about my moving in on her.

"That's ridiculous," she said.

"You really think so?"

"Of course I do." She took a deep breath. "Poor Will. Maybe his mother is right. Maybe something bad is going on out there. But maybe things are fine. Or maybe his father wants him to stay permanently, and Will's having difficulty deciding."

"I don't know about that."

She shrugged. "Neither do I," she said. "I hope not. I'd miss Will." She went over to the porch railing and sat down.

I dialed his number, but got the answering service.

I got up from the glider, put another tape on, and went over to Aphie.

"Your mother said you're not supposed to be on your feet. Get back there."

But I didn't. "Would you miss me if I left town?"

"What kind of a question is that?"

I shrugged.

"Let's dance," I said.

"You don't know how to."

"So teach me."

"You're not supposed to be on your feet." But she stood up. I put my arm around her waist and took her hand. Her hair tickled my ear, and her cheek felt so soft, I got dizzy. "Aphie," I said, "were you really upset when you thought I checked out this afternoon?"

"Checked out?"

"Died."

"I thought you wanted me to teach you how to dance."

"Well, were you?"

"Yes."

"Does that mean you like me?"

"I've always liked you," she said. "Well, almost always."

"Do you like Will better?"

"What do you mean?"

"You know."

She shook her head.

"He thinks I moved in on him," I said.

"What are you talking about?"

"With you."

"Why does he think that?"

"Because he likes you. More than likes you. And you're here and he's there."

"He's my friend," she said. "A best friend. And I love him, but not like that."

She was quiet for a minute, and then she looked up

at me with a weird kind of smile. "If anyone did the moving in, I did."

"What do you mean?"

She pushed away from me just a little. "Your brains did depart with your hair. . . ."

She put her head back near my shoulder and hummed along to the music, and we kept dancing. Her hair was up against my nose, and I almost sneezed. She lifted her face. I kissed her cheek. Then I kissed her lips. Mine were dry. So dry, my bottom lip stuck to hers, just for a second, and I felt like I was going to break into a thousand pieces. But we kept dancing. And when the music stopped, she looked up at me and smiled.

"I better lie down," I said.

"Your mother is going to kill me. I am definitely not a good baby-sitter."

"Want to bet?" I said.

I wanted to kiss her again, but I was afraid to. Instead, I asked her to hand me the phone. "I'm going to try Will again." Still no answer. Just the dumb machine. "I wish he'd answer."

"Wait until later," she said, taking the phone from my hand. "It's earlier out there. Maybe they're at the pool or something."

"I doubt it. Not the way he was talking."

She reached over me to put the phone back. "Are you all right?"

"Why?"

"You look pale even with that tan," she said.

"I do?"

"You do." She reached into her pocket and took out her lipstick. She put a little on her lips, bent over, and before I knew what was happening, kissed my cheeks, then rubbed them quickly and said, "There. That's much better."

And it was. Much, much better.

The house was quiet when I woke up the next morning. By the way the sun was coming through the blinds, I could tell it was late. I didn't want to piss Mueller off now, when I was so close. I jumped out of bed and headed for the bathroom, but before I got there, my mother was at the bottom of the stairs, calling up. "Where do you think you're running to? The doctor said no strenuous activity for two days."

Geez, I'd forgotten. Aphie was going to tell Mueller I had the flu. She promised me she wouldn't tell him about my fainting. I could just imagine what the guys, and Mueller, would do with that one. "I'm fixing you breakfast. I'll take it up."

I hated breakfast in bed. And my mother's breakfasts were worse than my father's pancakes. But I knew it would be useless for me to tell her I wasn't hungry. Last night, she kept coming in every few minutes asking me how I felt. The last time she did, my father stormed into my room, took her by the arm, and led her out. "You are not a nurse, Emily. And this is not a hospital where we wake the patients up to give them a sleeping pill."

The morning dragged. My brain kept flitting from one worry to another. Will. Mueller. The survival test.

The written test. Mr. Sozio. Mr. Krauss. Guilt over not telling my mother about him. And then at about three o'clock, Aphie called to tell me that Mueller had assigned times for the survival test and my name was on for Friday at noon.

"That's only five days away. Didn't you tell him I had the flu?"

"I did," she said. "But he couldn't have cared less."

"Shit."

"Watch your language."

"Sorry."

"How are you feeling?"

"Physically, fine. Mentally, lousy."

"What have you been doing?"

"Playing the guitar."

"Good. Have you heard from Will?"

"No. I've dialed that number about a hundred times. I don't even get the answering machine anymore. Just a bunch of clicks."

"I've been thinking that maybe they went down to Disneyland or something. It's not all that far away. I hope it's something like that," she said. "I'm going to go now. Mr Sozio will really be angry if neither one of us shows up."

"Wait. One minute. Did you miss me at practice?"

"Wel-l-l-l-l," she said, "yes. But I wasn't the only one."

"Who else?"

"All your girlfriends. You're the hero of Bayview Beach."

"You're kidding."

"Do I kid? I've got to go. See you later." Then she did something I'll remember till the day I die. "Catch these," she said. "Smack. Smack. Smack. Did you get them?" But before I could answer her, she hung up. I swear I could have floated away.

My mother had a few lessons, but every time one of them ended, she came out to the porch to check on me. Her last pupil was Miss Sullivan and when I saw her coming up the walk I pretended I was asleep.

"Faker," my mother whispered. And then she said, "Hello there, Alice. Today's the day we get to play a duet."

Just what I needed. A duet. My mother talked Miss Sullivan into the living room. "How's Mother? Oh, that's a pity. Arthritis can be awfully painful. Did you get to practice the sonata? . . ."

I tried covering my head with a pillow, but I could still hear the piano. And my mother. "Wonderful," she kept saying. "You are truly remarkable. Good. Keep going."

And then the duet. It didn't sound bad. I got up and stood at the living room window and watched. My mother was playing the bass line, Miss Sullivan the melody. She was swaying back and forth, smiling and nodding at Miss Sullivan. "Oh, my," my mother said, "this is fun. You're doing splendidly. Beethoven is a happy man today." And when the lesson was over, she talked Miss Sullivan down the porch steps. "Careful now. Watch that last step. Best regards to Mother. See you next week." And then she came back up the stairs, smiling.

170

She came over and felt my forehead for the forty-ninth time and said, "I'm going to make a meat loaf for supper. How does that sound?"

I must have fallen asleep because the next thing I knew Aphie was standing over me.

"How are you feeling?" she said.

"Okay."

"Ted, I went over to mow, but there was nothing to mow."

I sat up. "What do you mean nothing to mow?"

"I mean the whole place was mowed."

"Oh, geez," I said. "Sozio got somebody else, and there goes my money."

"No. Mr. Sozio didn't know anything about it. When I got there he told me what a beautiful job it was and to thank you for having somebody take care of it."

Then I knew the answer. I must have hit my head on the cement and cracked my skull when I fainted. All this was a dream. The grass was still there. Aphie wasn't here. And neither was I.

CHAPTER

23

Guilt's not my middle name anymore. It's my first. Dave, the guy from my father's lumberyard, had done the mowing for me. My father had told him what happened. ". . . and good old Dave drove his tractor mower over and took care of it. Doesn't want anything for it either."

And then there's my mother. "Your father told me the doctor said you were in excellent physical shape. That's the swimming," she said. "I'm proud of you. You've managed to swim, mow, keep up with Mr. Krauss. Everything."

"Mom," I said, "I've got to tell you something. . . ."

"Later, Ted," she said, waving her arm. "HELLO, THERE, MRS. STEIN. HOT ENOUGH FOR YOU . . . ?"

It was hot and getting hotter. I'd been sitting around

for almost two days now. The only thing my mother would let me do was play the guitar. Esme had given me some music and I fooled around with that. Dan had come over for a while this morning, and when I told him about the survival test, he told me not to worry about it.

"I've seen you in the pool. Relax." Then he told me exactly what I'd have to do. "You've got to float for a total of twenty minutes. Ten minutes each of hands only, then feet only."

"That's tough . . ."

"Sure, but you're up to it."

"Then you tread water for four minutes — two, arms only, two, legs only."

"Impossible."

"Then the quarter mile swim. You'll do fine," he said, picking up my guitar. "Want to hear what we're going to play for your parents' first dance?"

And then he played something so farty, it was hard to believe it could be anybody's favorite song. Even my parents'. "Remember," Dan said, "you're going to do the lead-in, then I'll come in with the piano. Then Esme takes over."

After he left, I wondered how I'd tell my mother about Krauss. One big problem was that I didn't have the money. Mr. Sozio was supposed to pay me, but I didn't know what he was going to do about that now. And I didn't know if Krauss would take me back. And there was always the possibility that she'd throw a fit and not let me finish up with Mueller. But the guilt was killing me. I mean really killing me.

And then there was Will. I still hadn't been able to get in touch with him, and when Mrs. Loughlin called to ask me how I was feeling, she said she hadn't heard from him either. "It's only a couple of days, but I'm getting anxious." Then she told me to take it easy and that she'd call if she heard from him.

At about four o'clock, the sun disappeared, and the air got very still. Mrs. Stein had left, and my mother was somewhere in the house. Aphie had come by earlier on her way over to do some clipping for Mr. Sozio. I asked her if she'd find out about my money. "You do it, Ted. You're the one who made arrangements with him." She was right. So I called him. He asked me how I felt and then he said, "Now we talk business." After we talked, he said he'd send my money with Aphie. "But I keep some back. You got to clip. Okay?"

Then I called Krauss. That was hard. So hard, I stuttered.

"Yes, yes," he said, "this is Mr. Krauss."

"This is T-T-Ted. I mean Theodore."

"So?"

And when I told him I wanted to come back, he said, "You are ready?"

"Yes, sir."

"You are sure?"

"I'm sure."

"You are not swimming?"

"No. I mean yes. I'm still swimming."

"But you are ready?"

"Yes, sir."

"Well, we'll see." He told me to come at two on Friday. "I see you then."

What could I say? I'm doing a survival swim at noon? I might not be able to use my arms at two? "Yes, sir," I said. "See you at two."

When I put the phone down, the biggest bolt of lightning and the loudest crack of thunder I ever heard came together. For a minute I thought it was a sign from God that I was finally doing things right. The wind came from nowhere and the porch blinds flapped like sheets. My mother came running out of the house.

"Get in the house, quick," she shouted as another bolt and crash came together.

I grabbed my guitar. My mother scooped up music and the telephone and we ran into the house. "Close the . . ." She didn't have to finish because the wind slammed the door shut.

She threw the music and the phone on the hall table and raced around, slamming windows shut. "Be right back," she said, running up the stairs. "I want to make sure everything is closed up."

"How about some tea?" she said when she had finished closing us in. I hate tea, but I said yes. And when the tea was ready, and we were sitting opposite each other at the kitchen table, I said, "Mom, I've got something to tell you."

"Do you want a piece of pie?" she asked, pouring me a cup of tea.

"Mom, listen to me. It's serious."

She looked up quickly. "You're not feeling dizzy, are you?"

I shook my head. "I'm fine," I said. "Mom, I haven't been taking lessons with Mr. Krauss."

"Excuse me?"

"I said I haven't been taking lessons from Mr. Krauss."

"What are you talking about?"

"He threw me out at the beginning of the summer because I wasn't practicing."

"But you've been going every week. And you've been practicing more than you ever have."

"That's so he'll take me back," I said. "I'm seeing him on Friday."

"Wait. Let me try to understand this," she said, a puzzled look on her face. "It's not my imagination that you've been going out of this house, guitar in hand, to go to Mr. Krauss's. I've seen it."

"I just took it so you'd think . . ." I felt worse telling it than I ever felt doing it.

She sat there, silent, sipping tea, shaking her head now and then. "I'm finding this hard to understand."

"It just happened."

She didn't answer me. The rain beat against the windows. I counted the seconds between the lightning and the thunder. I was up to fifteen before she spoke.

"Well," she said, "I . . ." She stopped. She put her cup to her lips, but didn't drink.

"The storm is at least fifteen miles away," I said, just to break the silence.

She put her cup down, clasped her hands together, looked at me, and, for a long time, said nothing. Then, her voice barely above a whisper, she said, "The storm is here." She put her cup down and slowly pushed it to the center of the table. I thought she was getting ready for the kill. But she laughed. She scared me. I thought it was hysteria and that she'd start crying and laughing at the same time.

"Mom, cut it out. Why are you laughing like that?"

She put her hand to her lips, still laughing, and said, "I'm thinking of something I saw in an old movie." She picked up a napkin and held it up to her face. "This boy lied to his father, or grandfather, I can't remember, but anyway, when it all came to light and the boy made his confession, he sat just the way you're sitting now, telling how sorry he was and how he'd never do it again." She blew her nose. " 'Does this mean I can't have my pony?' the little boy asked his father or whoever."

"Mom, I've got to do that survival on Friday. I've got to —"

"I am not finished," she said, in a hoarse whisper. She wiped around her eyes with the napkin and went on. " 'Well,' the father says, 'I think you've done penance enough. And I think you've learned your lesson.' "

I breathed again. "Thanks, Mom . . ."

"What do you mean, 'thanks, Mom?' I think it was the dumbest thing anybody ever said." She picked up her cup and saucer and walked over to the sink. She ran the water, rinsed them off, and put them in the dishwasher. Then she turned and said, "I am angry."

"I know, but . . ."

"And disappointed. Did it ever occur to you to tell me the truth?"

I didn't answer her.

"I might have understood."

I shrugged.

"But lying, Ted?" She reached up for her watering can. Whenever she's upset, she waters.

"I'm sorry I lied. I am. But I'm not sorry that I went for the swimming. I'm good at it."

She sighed and shook her head. "Your father is not going to be pleased."

"He knows."

She whirled around. "He what?"

"Yes."

"And he didn't tell me?"

"He wanted me to tell you."

She turned and ran the water into the watering can.

"And I have," I said. "And I'm sorry."

She stood on the kitchen stool and watered the plant over the sink. "That does not make everything okay, young man," she said, turning toward the plant on the refrigerator. I had the biggest urge to laugh because the way she was bending over with the spout of the watering can pointing the way it was, she looked like a circus elephant doing a trick on one of the those little stools.

I bit my lip. "Aphie's bringing your money later. Mr. Sozio paid me."

She turned. "I forgot about the money. Do you mean you spent it on something else?"

"I bought power tools so I could get the mowing done and still swim and practice guitar."

"Stop trying to evoke sympathy," she said. She got off the stool and watered every plant in the kitchen. When she finished, she went into the dining room to do the same. Then she came back into the kitchen and sat down, the watering can in her lap, and said nothing for a long, long time. Finally, she looked over at me. "Ted, I don't know what to say. And I'm disappointed in your father. He's never kept anything from me."

"I asked him to. He didn't want to. I swear he didn't."

"That doesn't excuse anything."

"Mom, I'll do anything, but please I'm begging —"

"Oh, stop it," she said. "I am not going to wave a magic wand and pretend all of this hasn't happened."

"I'll do anything. . . ."

"Keep still."

"But, Mom . . ."

"Look, Ted, I couldn't care less about your becoming a lifeguard."

"Mom," I said, "I'll get down on my knees. . . ."

She got up and went to the sink. She filled the watering can and put it on the counter. "I'll talk to your father about this."

I went over and said, "Mom, you don't know what this means —"

"Will you sit down and let me finish? Let's get something straight. You are not walking away from this as though it never happened."

"Anything. I'll do anything."

"But I'm too upset right now to decide what I'm going to do."

"Mom, you won't regret it. I'm going to win. I'm going to make all of you so proud."

"Stop it. You ought to know by now that I'm proud of you, but not for that. And certainly not for the lying." Then she turned to me. "And make no mistake, Ted, you are not getting a pony with no penance."

CHAPTER

24

"Way to go," Mueller yelled to me. "You're doing okay, Bradford. That was a terrific butterfly turn. Good show." With only two days to go before the survival test, I was doing great. I had successfully completed a one-person drag and a piggyback carry before I attempted the butterfly turn. It was getting easier all the time.

"Remember," Mueller warned when practice was almost over, "you've all got your slotted time for the survival part of the test. But be here when your time comes, or you are out. O. U. T. Out. No excuses. No exceptions."

He picked up his bullhorn. "Hey, you, Howe. Move your butt." Then he said, "The written test is on Monday. Then CPR starts on the twenty-second for those of you who pass both the survival and written tests. And then you can call yourselves lifeguards."

"Whoop-de-do," Denson said. Ever since I beat his time, he was putting down everything Mueller said. And when Mueller called his name, Denson turned to me. "How about if I practice the one-person drag with you?"

"Didn't you hear Mueller say you're doing it with Marty?"

"I was hoping he'd team me up with Lori." He leaned over toward me. "Her balloons would keep us floating in mud."

"You better not let Smiddy hear you talk like that."

"Are you for real? He's ready to dump her."

"But I saw him with her again this morning."

"You got some growing up to do, pal," he said.

Aphie came out of the water and when she spotted me she yelled, "Ted, bring me my towel. I'm freezing."

I headed toward Aph's blanket. Denson followed. "Have you done it with her yet?" he said.

"Hey," I said, turning to face him, "watch what you say about her."

"Touchy. Touchy."

"I mean it, Ray. Keep your mouth shut when it comes to her."

"Hey, chill out, buddy boy. I'm just fooling around." He put his arm around me.

I pulled away. "I got to go."

"So do I," he said, motioning to Marty. "Duty calls."

"Ray," I said, "I mean it. Don't talk like that about her again. Or even Lori."

"Who are you, Saint Theodore the First?"

"No. But . . ."

"Oh, go say a rosary, Goody Two-Shoes." He went over to say something to Marty, then turned and looked at me, and the two of them laughed.

I started to say, "With friends like you, a guy doesn't need enemies," but I stopped myself. It figures that the one time I thought of something smart, I didn't want to say it. I just turned my back and walked down toward Aph.

Mueller was behind his bullhorn again. "Attention. I'm going to say this once. Study your manuals. I want you to know every rule in chapter six. Tomorrow report at seven sharp. And be ready to do some heavy headwork."

"I guess he's staying home," I whispered to Aph, putting her towel around her shoulders.

She must have remembered the time Will had said that because her smile was kind of sad.

That was the only thing I didn't feel good about. Will. Aphie had gotten a postcard from him a couple of days after I talked to him. All it said was, "Hi. Having a good time. Weather is great." Not even, "Wish you were here." He'd talked to his mother, but I hadn't heard from him at all. I'd even stopped trying to call him.

Aphie had eased up on that. She wasn't pushing me to call him to find out what was going on. She even told me I should try not to worry and that maybe he *was* having a good time. But I wasn't convinced. I kept remembering what Will had told me: "When you're lying, you've got to keep it simple."

I had promised Mr. Sozio I'd finish up the clipping and as soon as Mueller let us go, Aphie and I took off. When we got there, we went into Will's apartment, but his mother wasn't home. Will's grandmother couldn't remember if Will had called that morning or not. And Marietta asked Aph about a thousand times if she knew Loretta Young.

We clipped the whole place in about two hours. Between what Dave had done and the electric clipper, it was a cinch. When we finished, we took a swim in the pool and ate our lunch.

I didn't want to get overtired, so I pulled out a couple of lounges from the pool house. It was early afternoon and the sun was hot. I pushed my lounge into the shade, and then moved Aphie's beside it. We lay side by side.

After a while Aph asked me what I was thinking about.

"Nothing."

"Not Will?"

"Not really."

"Friday?"

"Maybe. A little." But I was really thinking about her. It still amazed me that she really liked me. We'd been hanging around since kindergarten and all she ever did was boss me around and tell me what I was doing wrong, and now, all of a sudden, it was differ-

184

ent. Geez, it took Esme all of two hours to fall for Dan. Life confused me at times.

I turned and looked at her. "I'm thinking about you," I said. "You're different."

"Is that a compliment?"

"You know it is."

She laughed.

"Do you see a little change in me?" I said, remembering what she'd said at the beginning of the summer.

She nodded. "There's hope." Then she sat up. "It's too hot. I'm going for a swim."

I went after her. We swam for a while, then got some rafts and took turns tipping each other over.

"I'd better get going," she said, after a while. "My mother is *not* pleased with me. I'm supposed to get the house pulled together before my grandmother comes Friday."

We paddled the length of the pool on the rafts and when we got to the end, I pulled her raft over to me. I kissed her. Twice. And then without saying a word, she pushed me into the water, swam to the ladder, and got out.

"Why'd you do that?"

"Because I felt like it. And because I've got to get home. My mother, remember?"

We got our things together and just as we were leaving, Mr. Sozio came out. "How you feel?" he said.

I wanted to tell him that after kissing Aph I felt like flying, but all I said was, "Fine, thanks."

"That's good."

"Tomorrow you got the big day?"

"No, Mr. Sozio. Friday."

"Have some starch tomorrow night."

"Starch?" I said.

"Pasta. Like the athletes."

And when Aph and I were ready to leave, he said, "Remember, starch. Plenty of starch."

I remembered. And I swear I thought I was going to explode after dinner on Thursday night. I couldn't lie down; all I could do was sit in a chair.

"Don't worry," my father said. "You're not on until noon. By then you'll have digested it. If not, I'll get a stomach pump."

25

I didn't sleep much and as soon as the weakest light came into my room, I got out of bed and went downstairs. The kitchen was dark. The house was still; not a sound. I went outside. The grass was soft and damp, but I got down and did push-ups. I must have done a thousand because when I was finished, the yard was filled with light.

"Ted!" I heard my father call. "How are you feeling? Stomach okay?"

"Fine."

"Good. Come in and have something to eat."

When I got to the kitchen, he was pouring cereal into a bowl. "I'll make you pancakes tomorrow," he said, putting the bowl at my place.

He poured himself some coffee, sat down, and

opened the paper. I finished up the cereal and got myself some juice.

"Have a banana," he said. "You'll need the potassium."

"How do you know that? That's what Mueller said we should eat."

"I took Sports Etiquette 101," he said. "I kept clapping when I should have been booing. It got embarrassing." He looked over at me and laughed. "Everybody knows about potassium. Even your father."

"Too bad Mom didn't take it, too," I said, tossing a crumpled napkin at him. I took the banana and went back upstairs to lift the weights my father had bought for me. Then I lay down for a while. I must have fallen asleep because when I opened my eyes, my father was standing in the doorway all dressed.

"Better get up," he said.

"I'm nervous."

"Good. It'll keep you revved up," he said. "See you at dinner. And good luck."

My mother and Esme were still sleeping. I called Aphie but there was no answer, so I went back to my room and took out the manual to read over some of the stuff I thought I'd have to know. Then I pulled out my guitar, went out to the backyard, and started to play. My fingers weren't stiff anymore — they really moved — but I couldn't concentrate. My head was at the beach. And my stomach was jumping around.

"Ted," I heard my mother call, "do you want me to fix you some eggs? It's almost nine."

"Nine o'clock?" I looked at my watch. It *was* almost nine. Only three hours to go. "No, thanks," I said. "I'll fix something light."

"Well, come on in and fix it. You don't want to eat much later than this."

I spread some peanut butter on a banana and headed for the shower. I let the hot water beat on the back of my legs to loosen them up. I said a couple of prayers, and just as I was about to make a deal with God, I heard my mother call me.

"I can't hear you," I yelled. "Talk louder."

She opened the door a bit.

"Hey, close that —"

"Oh, stop it. I can't see anything in here, it's so steamy. Will's on the phone."

"Now he calls," I said under my breath. "I'm soaked. Get his number. I'll call him back."

I soaped myself all over and was just about to rinse myself off when my mother banged on the door. "He's in a phone booth. He says he has to talk to you."

"Cripes, just what I need." I wrapped a towel around me. "I'll be right out."

My mother was waiting, the phone in her hand.

"I've got to get going. . . ."

"Shhhh," she said, giving me the phone.

"Hey, Will, where the hell have you been?"

"Ted," my mother said, "watch that."

"Manhattan? *The* Manhattan?" I almost dropped the phone. "How come? Where in Manhattan?" I felt like somebody had kicked me in the stomach when Will told me where he was.

"Wait a minute," I said. I put my hand over the mouthpiece, and spoke to my mother. "He's at Penn Station in a phone booth. He's crying."

"Where's his father?"

"Where's your father?" I repeated to Will. "How come he didn't —"

I looked over at my mother. "He left for Paris yesterday." I put my hand back over the receiver. "They never went to Seattle. They were in Manhattan the whole time."

"Did he call his mother?"

I took my hand off and said, "Does your mother know?"

"I don't want her to know," he yelled into the phone. "Don't tell her."

I looked back at my mother and shook my head. "Okay. Okay. Calm down. What are you going to do?"

"I don't have any money."

"You mean he left you with no money?"

"I threw it back at him. I don't want anything."

"That wasn't very smart."

"I don't need this shit."

"Sorry. I'm sorry. But what do you want me to do?"

"I thought maybe bring me some money. . . ."

"I'm supposed to be at the beach by —"

"So go," he shouted. "Forget I asked."

"Hey, calm down. Let me think."

I put my hand over the receiver and looked over at my mother. "He needs money. If I go now I'm going to miss my time."

She didn't say anything.

"Can you go? Please?"

She shrugged, then said, "I guess . . . but what about his mother?"

I shook my head and took my hand off the receiver. "It's all set, buddy," I said. "My mother is coming."

"No way," he yelled. "Forget it. No damned way do I want that —"

"Please deposit eighty-five cents for an additional five minutes," the operator said.

"I'm getting out of here. . . ."

"No," I yelled. "Don't. Don't hang up. Tell me where you are. I'll come. But don't hang up. I'll be there. Only don't hang up."

He didn't answer for a minute. Then he said, his voice breaking, "I'll see you at the information booth."

"Which one?"

"Long Island."

I hung up. And if I live to be a thousand I hope I never again feel the way I did then. Because most of me wanted to get on my bike and get to the beach. And only a little part of me was holding me back from not doing it.

I headed back to the bathroom to rinse off the soap. "Will you ask Esme to take me to the station?"

"She's not here," my mother said. "Dan picked her up."

"Can you call Dad?"

"He had an appointment in Deerfield this morning."

"Oh, geez . . ."

"Don't worry. I'll think of something."

I got dressed and when I was ready, my mother was standing in the kitchen with the car keys in one hand, her pocketbook in the other.

"What are you doing? You can't drive."

"I certainly can. I just don't have a license."

She got into the car and told me to guide her out of the driveway. "Now, don't be nervous," she said.

She turned on the ignition. "Is anybody coming?"

I ran down the driveway and looked both ways. "Come on," I said. "But be careful."

The car shot toward the garage. I ran up and stuck my head in the window. "Put it in reverse, Mom," I said, pointing to the R on the dashboard.

"Okay," she said, peering over the wheel to make sure she put it in the right gear. "I'm off."

"Wait," I shouted, running down the driveway again. And when I gave the all clear, she started down.

She inched down the driveway, the car bouncing every time she hit the brake, but she made it to the street. I ran and got in the front seat.

"See? Didn't I tell you I could drive?"

She drove down Shore Road about five miles an hour and when she started to talk, I said, "Mom, maybe you'd better concentrate on the road. It's your first time out."

"And probably my last," she said, stopping at a red light. "I don't like driving. And at my age I try not to do anything I don't like to do."

When we finally got to the station, the next train to

192

go out was the 10:05. We had about five minutes to wait. My mother handed me two twenty-dollar bills. "He'll be hungry." She looked at me. "Don't think I don't know what you're feeling. I know how much today meant to you."

After a second or so, she reached over and squeezed my hand. "You're doing your penance. And more."

She kissed my cheek and for a second I felt like burying my face on her shoulder and letting go. I took a deep breath and then we just sat, the silence filling the car. When the train pulled in, I kissed her and got out and walked toward the train. "Be careful, Ted," she called.

"You be careful going home. You just made your maiden voyage. Take it slow and easy."

"I will."

The train was packed. I took a seat on the left, away from the bay side. I didn't want to see it when the train went over the trestle. But my mind pictured what my eyes couldn't see. I could even hear Mueller yelling orders. I picked up a newspaper somebody had left and tried to concentrate. When the conductor announced that everybody had to change at Jamaica, I got up and stood by the door.

I had to wait at Jamaica about twenty minutes before the train to Manhattan came in. It was tough waiting by myself. I really tried not to think of what was going on down at the beach. Denson passed, I knew that. Aphie, too, no doubt of that.

All that practice for nothing. Today was going to be

my big day. The day everybody was going to see me ending up like some kind of hero. And here I was waiting at Jamaica.

"LOCAL TO NEW YORK/PENN STATION ON TRACK FOUR," a voice over the loudspeaker called. "EXPRESS TO BAYVIEW ON TRACK SIX. LAST CALL."

It was a short walk over to Track Four, but it seemed to take me forever to get there.

CHAPTER

26

Will wasn't at the information booth when I got there. I walked around the booth for a while, thinking he'd spot me from wherever he was. But he didn't. Even now he was late. I walked in and out of the stores, thinking maybe he needed a men's room. But the stores didn't have them, so I walked around the station until I spotted one. I pushed the door open a little and said, "Hey, Will, you in there?" And when somebody said, "Get lost. There ain't nobody in here but me," I panicked, thinking about how people get beaten up in rest rooms all the time.

"Can I have somebody paged?" I said, when I got back to the information booth.

"You lost?"

"No, I was supposed to meet somebody here a while back. . . ."

He pointed to another area. "Have a look in the waiting room. If she's not there, I'll page her." He winked at me. "Maybe she spotted somebody else. Like a movie star. We get a lot of them big stars around here." He looked over at the other guy in the booth and said, "Don't we?"

"You said it, Al," the other guy said. "Just the other day who should poke his nose through my window but Mickey Mouse."

Al was right; Will was in the waiting room. He was sitting facing the wall, his head down, his duffel bag at his feet. I walked over to him very slowly. "Hey, Will! How's it going?"

He didn't answer.

"Sorry it took so long, but the train was slow, and then I think I got off somewhere in Hoboken. . . ."

He didn't even look at me.

I sat down beside him. "You okay?"

He didn't answer.

I was quiet for a while and then I said, "There's a train back home at eleven fifty-eight."

He shook his head.

"Okay," I said. "It's okay. We'll take one later."

And then we just sat.

"EXPRESS TO PORT LUCIE ON TRACK NINE-TEEN," the loudspeaker boomed.

Now I know what my mother means when she says, "You don't know where you're going to be from one minute to the next." I used to think it was a crazy thing to say, but here I was, sitting in the waiting room at Penn Station. But my mind wasn't with my body. I

196

was picturing myself up in that tower again. My body tanned and slick with oil . . .

"Hey, you," a crazy-looking guy sitting across from me yelled, "what are you staring at?" He pointed to me. "I'm talking to you."

"I wasn't staring. . . ."

He jumped up. "You want to stare? I'll give you something to make your eyes pop." He grabbed his throat. "I'm a fish in the East River," he said, his eyes bulging. Then he gagged, flapped his arms, and fell on the floor. "I'm every fish in the East River," he said, stretching out like he was dead.

"EXPRESS TO NEWTONVILLE ON TRACK TWENTY-ONE."

He jumped up, pushed his hat against my chest, and said, "For ecology."

I fumbled through my pockets, grabbed some change, and threw it in.

"I thank you," he said, bowing, "and so do the fish."

"Hey, Will," I said, when the guy got out of earshot. "Did you see that? We'd better get going." But Will wasn't where his body was either.

I waited a while and then said, "I'm going to get you something to eat. You want milk or juice?"

He shrugged.

"Juice. I'll get juice. The milk is probably sour."

I didn't feel hungry, and when I got back I handed Will a napkin and pulled a chocolate doughnut out of the bag. "Your favorite." Then I passed him the juice. "I've got more in the bag."

He kind of picked at the doughnut, but drained the juice. I gave him mine.

"Thanks," he said.

"You're welcome."

"LAST CALL FOR THE 11:44 TO PORT LUCIE LEAVING ON TRACK NINETEEN."

"About the other day . . ." he started to say.

"Forget it," I said.

". . . it wasn't you. . . ."

"It's okay, Will. We're buddies."

Then he reached out. I took his hand. Will and I never do stuff like that. But I held on. His hand was cold in mine and his shoulders shook.

"Are you cold?"

He nodded.

I took off my sweatshirt and put it around him.

"He's a liar and a cheat," Will said. "He lies to everybody. He doesn't know what it means to be honest with anyone."

A huge sob came from somewhere deep inside him.

"He feeds off people." He looked at me, his eyes red, his nose running. I handed him another napkin.

"There's nothing inside him." He looked away. "You know?"

I didn't answer. I knew I didn't need to.

"It's like he's a body, just a body. Like one of those mannequins." He blew his nose. "I swear to you, he's got no feelings." Then he looked back at me. "He didn't want me."

I kept quiet. I didn't want to say some stupid thing

that wouldn't mean anything. So I just put my arm around him.

"Why did he ask me to come?"

I shrugged and shook my head.

"I hate him." His voice was hoarse, his shoulders quivering. "I hate my own father."

"Everybody does sometimes."

He looked straight at me. "You've got no right to. Your father's a good guy. A real good guy."

I looked at him, thinking of all the times Will had been there for me without my asking. Like the night we thought my father had had a heart attack. Will kept insisting it was the chicken. "It's food poisoning," he said. "Same thing happened to my grandmother." That got me through the night. And the time old man Shearer accused me of cheating on a math exam. Will was the only one who stood up for me. Shearer backed down, but he hated Will after that.

"I know he's a good guy," I said. "Just like you."

And then he really broke down. I kept my arm around him. We sat there for a long time and when Will finally got hold of himself, I asked him if he was ready to go home.

He nodded.

"Your mom's been worried. Did you talk to her?"

He shook his head. "I don't want her to know. This is just between you and me."

"Hey, Will," I said, "there's some stuff you can't stop from happening. She's going to find out. She probably knows already."

"Not from me."

"And me either. But that's not going to stop her from knowing. It's like Christmas. You can't stop it from coming. It just happens. And that's the way things like this are."

He looked at me with a funny smile.

"What's that for?"

"Because you sound so old. Like Aphie."

"You know, Will, about Aphie . . ."

"I'm sorry I said what I said."

"It wasn't true, Will. What you said about me moving in on her. At least not then. But things change. . . ."

"Some things," he said.

I knew what he was saying but I didn't have an answer.

"It's okay," he said. "Better you than somebody like Denson." He smiled. "Honest. It's okay."

"But I want you to know . . ." I wanted to tell him that I really didn't make the first move. I wanted to tell him how surprised I was that Aph liked me that way, but then I thought it wouldn't be the thing to do. Not now, anyway.

". . . that the next train leaves in about fifteen minutes. But you're calling your mom first. Understand? You've got to tell her and it'll be easier to do on the phone without your grandmother and Marietta."

"And Loretta . . ."

"Yeah," I said, laughing. "Definitely without Loretta."

200

I got some change and we headed over to a telephone. He picked up the receiver and dialed. And when he said, "Mom, it's Will. I'm on my way home," I heard the noon whistle blow.

CHAPTER

27

As soon as Will hung up, I said, "Hey, tell me something, how could you have been in Manhattan when I talked to you in Seattle?"

"He's got this special phone service," Will said. "No matter where he is, everybody thinks he's in Seattle." He shook his head. "I swear, when it comes to conning people, he knows every trick there is. Every single one."

I gave him a shove. "Come on. I'm buying lunch." I bought two sausage hero sandwiches and a half gallon of grape juice, and we headed down to the train. We took two seats across from each other, hoping nobody would sit next to us. Nobody did.

Will wolfed down his hero and half of mine before the train left Penn Station. Then he started on the juice.

"Hey," I said, "leave me a little." And when he wouldn't stop drinking, I yanked it out of his hand.

He pulled it back. I yanked it back again. Will pulled and I yanked and when I did, the container burst open and went all over us.

I took one look at Will and started to laugh. He had grape juice dripping down his nose and onto his pants. "You look like you took a purple piss."

He laughed so hard, he could barely talk. "You should talk," he said, pointing to my head. "You look like Mr. Potato Head checking out of brain surgery."

The conductor told us to quiet down, checked our tickets, and told us to change at Jamaica.

"Hey," I said, after we'd calmed down, "you ever hear the joke about the guy who rides the Long Island Railroad every day?"

"Is it clean?"

"Nathaniel told me this one so it's got to be clean."

"Why tell it then?"

"It's funny. You'll like it. This guy changed trains at Jamaica every day for forty years. One day he's running for the train and he drops dead. When he gets to heaven, Saint Peter's waiting for him at the Pearly Gates. 'You can't come in yet,' Saint Peter says. 'You'll have to go to Purgatory for a while.' So the guy says, 'That's fine with me, but do I change at Jamaica?'"

"That's funny?"

"I thought so when he told me."

"You must have been around three."

"No, actually, I was two. I've got a good memory."

"That was funnier than the joke."

"Thank you, sir."

"You want to hear something really funny?"

"Is it clean?"

"My father told me he probably will be living in Paris for good."

"That's funny?"

"He told me he'd treat me to Christmas in Paris. Tell me that's not funny?"

"Would you go?"

"Yeah, sure," Will said. "I'll get Santa to take me."

He put his head back and closed his eyes. After a while, he fell asleep. He got that dopey expression he gets when he sleeps and his mouth drops open. He looked like a real little kid. Almost like he did that day when we were eleven, and we came home from the ball game alone. I remembered how that lady had thought I was Will and how his dad didn't tell her she was wrong. Neither did Will.

I could just hear me if my father did something like that, which he wouldn't. He'd have put his arm around me and said something like, "This one's my son." And then probably he'd have put his other arm around Will and said, "And this is his friend."

"J-a-a-maica, next," the conductor said. "Stay on for Pleasant Point and Ocean City. Everybody else, change at Jamaica."

I nudged Will awake. We got our things together and waited by the door.

"TRAIN TO BAYVIEW ON TRACK THREE."

We dashed out the door and over to the train. It was jammed but we finally found an empty seat in the last

204

car. Will asked me to take the window. "I get sick to my stomach when I look at the tracks going by."

He threw his bag up on the rack and sat down. "Today was the big day," he said, his face serious, his voice soft.

I nodded.

"I didn't know. I wouldn't have called."

"I know."

"You can make it up."

"No," I said, "you know Massive."

"Tell him what happened."

"Hey, Will, it doesn't matter."

"Who are you kidding?"

"I probably wouldn't have done too good sitting up in one of those towers anyway," I said. "I'm afraid of heights."

"You're a liar."

"I'm serious."

"And I'm Pinocchio and you're Jiminy Cricket."

"And Mueller is the whale. . . ."

"And you're full of crap."

"Watch your language, Will," I said, trying to imitate Aphie's voice.

I looked out the window as trees whizzed by and colors blurred. The wind coming through the open window made my eyes burn. My throat ached so I took a big breath and let it out, then turned to Will. "You know something?" I said. "Growing up stinks. It really does."

Will nodded. "Don't I know it," he said. "Boy, don't I know it."

"Next stop Ashton," the conductor called out. "Then express to Bayview."

The train arrived early and Will's mom wasn't there yet. We fooled around on the platform, me doing a Muhammad Ali imitation. A jab here. One there. A right to the shoulder. And then I told Will how pretty I was. That cracked him up.

"Bradford," he said, "you're crazy."

"Speaking of crazy, guess who took me to the station this morning?"

"Esme?"

"My mother."

"Your mother?"

"Fact," I said. "You should have seen her. Sitting up like somebody was pulling her head through the roof. Rigid. Looking straight ahead. Going about four miles an hour." I stopped. "But she was great. She'll never do it again. But she was great."

"And I missed it," Will said.

"Yeah," I said. "You missed it."

It was getting really hot, so we decided to walk through the park toward the entrance where his mother would be coming in. It was almost one-thirty. The testing was all over down at the beach. Denson would be strutting around like he always does, his buddies following him, a million girls surrounding them. And Mueller would be buying everybody burgers and Cokes, the way he promised he would.

When we got to the entrance, we sat under a shade tree. There was a little breeze and the air felt cool. In the distance we could see another train heading into

Manhattan. Will turned to me and said, "Thanks, Ted."

"Nothing to it," I lied.

Will's mom pulled into the entrance and we walked over to meet her. And when we got there, I turned to Will. "The next time you pull something like this, you know what I'm going to do?" Before he could answer, I said, "I'm going to send my hair for you. The hair cable. The one you told me would grow thirty-seven miles long."

28

This morning I went down to the bay. I set my alarm for five o'clock, but I was awake long before that. I got dressed, stuffed my swimming gear into my duffel bag, and waited for the first light to come through the window. Everybody was asleep so I crept across the hall, down the stairs, and out to the garage. I walked my bike down the driveway and took off. The air was cool and there was a light fog coming in off the water. The road was deserted. Seagulls were heading into shore. "Storm coming," I could hear my father say.

I stuck to the middle of the road and thought about yesterday. How I'd told Will's mom I wasn't feeling too good when she'd asked me to come home with them. The truth was I hadn't wanted to see anybody. Not Aphie. Not anybody. I hadn't wanted to hear all the stuff I knew I'd hear about Denson and the rest of them.

When I reached the bay, the horizon was barely visible. The tide was on its way out and a breeze floated over the bay, rippling the water just a little. There was an old fishing barge offshore. I figured that out to where the barge was anchored and over to the dock should be just about a quarter of a mile.

I took off my shirt and pants and ran in the sand for five. And then the weirdest thing happened. I swear I heard somebody yelling to me to take another five. I looked around, but nobody was there.

Take another five.

So I did.

You're on, Bradford. Get set.

I stopped running and toweled the sweat from my face. I shook my hands and did a few knee bends. Then I got into position. Hands on my knees. Right foot behind my left.

Ready?

"Ready," I called out, checking to make sure my watch was on tight.

Twenty-yard underwater swim. Get set. Go!

I raced to the shore, into the water, and dove in. I swam underwater and when I was pretty sure I'd done twenty yards I surfaced.

Float for twenty. Ten, hands only. Ten, feet only.

I moved my hands to keep me floating. No sweat. I checked my watch and then used only my legs. My body didn't fight me. It did just what I wanted it to do.

Tread for four. Two, arms only. Two, feet only.
Quarter-mile swim next. Lifesaving stroke first.

I slid across the water. My breathing was smooth. My head stayed close to the surface. My feet kicked, still feeling like they had a tiny outboard attached. My arms pushed me forward. I was part of the water.

Breaststroke.

Approach crawl.

Finish it up with a backstroke.

I flipped over. My arm shot out of the water. Back in. Other arm out. In.

The clouds started to break. I rounded the fishing barge. I felt light. Free. I kept going.

That's it. Come on in.

But I didn't. Not then. I flipped over. My head stayed close to the water, my feet did double time. My arms dug in and pushed me forward, faster and faster. The only sound I heard was the water rushing past my ears. I passed the barge again. I flipped onto my back and floated. The clouds were gone; the sky was bright. I floated toward shore and when I was almost there, I turned and swam as fast as I could.

The water warmed up as I got near shore, and when I felt the ground beneath me, I leaped up like a dolphin at feeding time and turned to face the bay. The sun was just breaking out of the water. "Hey," I shouted, "I did it. Me. Ted Bradford. I did it."

Then I toweled myself dry, got dressed, and hopped on my bike. Shore Road was still deserted and I rode alone until a flock of Canada geese appeared from nowhere and flew above me in perfect formation. For a while, we rode the road together, but after a while, they moved ahead. I pedaled faster trying to keep up, but fell behind. I made the turn into my road and when I did, I saw them turn and head in the opposite direction.

Everybody was still sleeping when I got home. I grabbed a box of cookies and a couple of bananas and went back upstairs. I pulled my guitar from the closet, tuned it, and played it real soft. And when I smelled coffee coming up from the kitchen, I went out to the phone and called Will. "Hey, Loughlin," I said, "get your tail over here. I'm going to get my dad to make us a mess of pancakes."

29

Denson didn't pass the written test. I couldn't believe it. I felt kind of sorry for him, because the way I figure it now, he needs that tower more than I do. But every once in a while, even knowing what I know now, I think how great it would have been if there had been a crowd on the beach the morning that I passed the survival test. I guess it's that same part of me that wanted the tower so bad with all the girls looking up at me and my oiled chest. The part of me that didn't want to go into Manhattan to bring Will home. But nobody's perfect. My hair sure isn't. Aphie cut the tail off, but it still looks pretty bad.

Aphie passed everything. I knew she would. She made the best time, but you'd never know it. She never brags. She told me she was going to wait and take the

CPR course next year. "That way, we can take it together." But next summer is so far off.

Dave asked me if Will and I would like to buy his tractor mower. "I'm getting a bigger one. Give you a good buy." Will and I thanked him, but decided we'd better not. "Who knows what T and W Lawn Services will be doing next summer?" Will said. "Maybe we'll travel. Maybe stop off in Paris for a day or two." I didn't know if Will was serious or not, so I shut up.

And Mr. Krauss told me he was going to recommend me for a summer scholarship up at Tanglewood. This summer I would have died before I'd do something like that. But when he told me, all I could say was, "You're kidding."

"I do not kid, Theodore," he said.

I'll see about that, too. I'd miss Aphie. "You two are an item," Denise Doherty said the other day. Like we're specials in the supermarket. Aphie's not an item in the supermarket, but she is special. I swear Will was right about her looking like Snow White. But that's not what makes her special. It's what's inside. What makes her Aphie and nobody else. That sounds like something my mother would say, but it's how I feel. We haven't done it, or anything like that, but when I'm with Aph, I feel great. She still acts about ninety-five once in a while, but she's getting better.

I'd miss Will, too. I didn't realize how much I'd missed him till he came back. Or maybe I was the one who came back. I didn't mention it, but Will had lost a lot of weight when he was with his Dad. He looks great. He's been getting a lot of attention from the girls. The cute ones. But he's not interested. He and Josette Gormley have got this thing going. Her braces are off and she even got a violin case with enough room for her bow. She asked Will if she could be his date for my parents' party.

Esme and I had a thousand arguments before the party. She kept inviting people, like we were millionaires or something. She invited everybody from the lumberyard and all my mother's pupils. Even Mr. and Mrs. Krauss. When I complained about the guest list being so huge and so weird she told me to mind my own business. "It is my business," I said. "I'm helping to pay for it."

But all she'd say was, "Go practice the music. Especially their song."

Their song. What a drag. Will and I practiced every day. Will is good. He really can make those sticks fly. But even so, and even though Dan jazzed up some of the music for the party, it was still pretty futzy. The music. Not the party.

The party was great. Nathaniel surprised my parents by coming in from California. But the biggest surprise was the way my parents acted that night. I never saw people have such a good time. They danced like they were fifteen years old. My father thanked everybody for coming. He thanked his loyal employees. He thanked my mother's pupils for "enriching my Emily's life." He thanked my mother for being his wife for thirty years. "You're as beautiful today as you were then," he said, kissing her in front of everybody. He thanked Esme and Nathaniel and me "for being my children." He hugged and kissed us. It was embarrassing.

After my mother thanked everybody and did *her* kissing, Esme said we should play their song. I took the lead, and when my mother heard me, she put her hands up to her mouth and started to cry. My father went over and took her hand and led her onto the patio. And even though Esme was singing into the microphone, I could hear the two of them singing along. It really felt good to be playing for them.

You know, it's funny, Will and I practiced that song a thousand times and I never heard the words. But I heard them that night. I still remember them. And I remember my mother's smile and my father looking down at her. Esme and Dan announced that they were going to be engaged and that she'd be going out to Ohio with him. I thought my mother would take off for the moon. Or at least hire the caterer.

When the party was almost over, I danced with my mother. She led. She told me how proud she was of me. She was teary-eyed and it got embarrassing, especially when she whispered, "Lately I forget you're my baby." But I stuck it out until the music stopped. I even walked her back to her seat.

And when Dan played my parents' song for the last time, I played for a while before I put down my guitar and went over to ask Aphie to dance. She led, too. We danced okay for a while, not talking, and then the funniest thing happened. The two of us started to sing at the same time.

You've got to give a little, take a little,
and let your poor heart break a little.

Then my parents started to sing along with us.

You've got to laugh a little, cry a little
and let the clouds roll by a little.

Then Esme and Dan and Will and Josette, for crying out loud.

As long as there's the two of us,
we've got the world and all its charms . . .

Will's Mom started up and so did Miss Sullivan and Mrs. Stein. The Krausses and everybody else. Like a chorus, for God's sake.

. . . and when the world is through with us,
we've got each other's arms.

Then people started getting teary. Everybody kissed everybody else at least five times. I kissed Aphie once. But it was enough. And when everybody had kissed everybody else and only the music played, Aphie and I sang.

You've got to win a little, lose a little,
yes, and always have the blues a little
'cause that's the story of, that's the glory of love.
Yeah, that's the story of, that's the glory of love.